by Walter R. Brooks

Alfred A. Knopf: PUBLISHER

FREDDY *Goes To the* NORTH POLE

Freddy had an idea that the animals would like to travel, so he made himself president of Barnyard Tours, Inc.

The company grew to great proportions topped by Freddy leading Charles, Jinx, the Mesdames Wiggins and Wogus, and some others into a pack of polar problems in the Arctic regions where they visited for a while with Santa Claus.

"Is that someone singing?"

FREDDY

Goes To the

NORTH POLE

by WALTER R. BROOKS

Originally published as
MORE TO AND AGAIN

THE OVERLOOK PRESS
WOODSTOCK & NEW YORK

First published in the United States in 2001 by
The Overlook Press, Peter Mayer Publishers, Inc.
Lewis Hollow Road
Woodstock, NY 12498
www.overlookpress.com

Library of Congress Cataloging-in-Publication Data

Brooks, Walter R., 1886-1958.
[More to and again]
Freddy goes to the North Pole / Walter R. Brooks ; illustrated by Kurt Wiese.
p. cm.
Previously published as: More to and again.
Summary: Freddy the pig and his barnyard friends run the very successful Barnyard
Tours, Inc., but on a trip to the North Pole some sailors cause trouble for them and
Santa, who, when the animals drive off the bad men, offers a sleigh ride home.
[1. Pigs—Fiction. 2. Travel—Fiction. 3. Domestic animals—Fiction. 4. Santa Claus—
Fiction. 5. Adventure and adventurers—Fiction.] I. Wiese, Kurt, 1887- ill. II. Title.
PZ7.B7994 Frck 2001   [Fic]—dc21   00-050151

Manufactured in the United States of America
ISBN 1-58567-104-5
1 3 5 7 9 8 6 4 2

Contents

CONTENTS

FREDDY *Goes To the* NORTH POLE

CHAPTER I
FREDDY HAS AN IDEA

JINX, the cat, was walking round in the bushes behind the barn, looking for excitement. Things had been very quiet on the farm for a long time. Nothing really interesting had happened since spring, when he and the other animals had come back from their trip to Florida. That had been a great trip! He purred whenever he thought of it.

Suddenly he crouched down and began to lash his tail. A little grey shape darted out from under the barn into the shadow of a bush. Noiselessly Jinx crept forward, inch by inch, until he was within jumping-distance. But just as he was about to spring, a little squeaky voice came from under the bush:

" Hey, Jinx! Stop it! It's me — Eeny! "

Jinx stopped crouching and straightened up. He gave a disgusted sniff. " I might have known it!" he growled. " There's never anything new around this place! Since I made friends with you and your family and promised to leave you alone, I haven't seen hide nor hair, nor tooth nor tail of anything I could hunt. Friendship's all very well, but it spoils lots of good sport."

" I'm sorry," said the mouse. He came out from the shadow and sat down beside Jinx and began to clean his whiskers with his fore-paws. " But you ought to be more careful, Jinx. You might have jumped on me and hurt me."

" How'd I know it was you? " said the cat. " You said your cousins were giving a party down in the pasture. I thought you'd be down there."

" I was," said Eeny. " But I came away early. It wasn't much of a party. Why, all they gave

4

us to eat was grass roots and a little birch bark. Even if they are my cousins, I *must* say — "

" Oh, don't tell me anything about relatives! " said Jinx. " I've got a dozen brothers and sisters in this neighbourhood, but if I was starving, d'you think any of 'em would give me as much as a robin's claw or a mouse tail — excuse me, Eeny."

The mouse shuddered slightly and curled his tail tightly under him. " Don't mention it," he said.

Jinx gave a loud laugh. " I won't — again," he said. " Come on, let's go down to the pig-pen and see what Freddy's doing."

As Jinx and Eeny walked side by side through the orchard, they met Mrs. Bean, the farmer's wife. Mrs. Bean had an empty bucket in her hand, because she had been feeding the pigs; and when she saw the two of them, she stared and stared. " Land sakes! " she exclaimed. " What this farm's coming to I don't know! When I was a girl, animals behaved the way you expected them to. Cats and mice didn't go out walking together and pigs didn't read newspapers and there weren't any of these animal parties given in the barn. It's more like a circus than a farm here ever since these animals got back from Florida last year. Here, Jinx! Come, kitty, kitty! "

Jinx walked over to her. He didn't want to, but Mrs. Bean liked him and was very good to him, so he was always polite to her. She petted him and scratched his head, and then she pointed to Eeny, who, while he waited for his friend, was nibbling at an apple that had fallen from one of the trees.

" Look, Jinx. Go chase the mouse. See? Nice fat mouse! M'm! Mice, Jinx, mice! "

Jinx crouched down and lashed his tail. " I'll have to chase you, Eeny," he said. " Run over towards the fence, and I'll pretend to look for you, and then we can go on down and see Freddy."

Eeny scurried off, squeaking with pretended fright, and Jinx, looking as ferocious as

6

possible, bounded after him. But as soon as they were out of sight of Mrs. Bean, they walked along again side by side.

" What did she mean about pigs reading newspapers? " asked Eeny.

" Oh," said Jinx, " that's Freddy. I've been teaching him to read and he's crazy about it. He reads everything he can lay his hoofs on now."

" Good gracious! " squeaked the mouse. " I didn't know you could read, Jinx."

" Read! " Jinx waved his tail importantly. " That's nothing. I can do anything I set my mind to. I learned to read sitting on Mrs. Bean's lap when she read the newspaper out loud to Mr. Bean."

As they came in sight of the pig-pen, they saw quite a group of animals sitting round in a circle outside, and in the middle of it was Freddy. He seemed to be reading aloud from a paper that lay on the ground in front of him, for whenever he said anything, all the others would either cheer or groan.

7

"Hurry up! He's reading the baseball news!" said Jinx, and started to run.

Eeny started to run too, but his legs were much too short to keep up with a cat. "Hey, Jinx, wait for me!" he shouted.

Jinx stopped. "Sorry," he said, and, picking up the mouse carefully in his mouth, bounded down into the middle of the circle, knocking over one or two of the smaller pigs as he did so. That was the way Jinx always did things. He had the best heart in the world, but he was apt to be rather rough and thoughtless.

"'Lo, Freddy, old scout," he said. "Who won yesterday?"

"The Giants," said the pig. "Very close game. Two and two at the end of the eighth inning, and then Whippenberger knocked a home run and brought two men in."

"Whippenberger?" said Jinx. "Who's he? That new shortstop? What's his batting average?"

"Oh my goodness!" said Freddy crossly. "You can read, Jinx. Why don't you look it up

8

yourself? I'm sick of doing the reading for all the animals on the farm. I don't get a chance to do anything I want to any more. Always somebody coming down here to get me to read something. And I'm especially sick of reading all these long accounts of baseball games. Maybe you get some fun out of it, but I don't. What's the sense of getting all excited about a game played by somebody else — a game that we animals couldn't play ourselves if we wanted to? I think it's silly."

Freddy was usually so cheerful and good-natured that all the other animals were very much surprised at this outburst, and they just sat and stared at him without saying anything. But Jinx said:

" Maybe you're right, Freddy. I'd a lot rather go out and have adventures of my own than sit home and read about those somebody else had. Look at the fun we had going to Florida. Wasn't that better than reading a book about it? "

" Yes, yes. Oh my, I should say so! "

9

exclaimed Freddy and Eeny and Robert, the dog. They and Jinx were the only ones there who had taken the Florida trip, and they naturally felt a little superior to the other animals on that account and were sometimes inclined to put on airs about it. And Ferdinand, the crow, who lived in the woods, had a very exasperating habit of sitting up in the big elm near the barn, where all the animals could hear him, and puffing out his chest and saying importantly: " Well, when I was in Florida — " And then he would burst into a loud derisive laugh.

So now, as soon as the subject of Florida was brought up, all the other animals groaned and walked away, leaving Freddy and Eeny and Jinx and Robert alone.

" I mean what I said, Jinx," said Freddy. " We ought to be doing something ourselves, instead of reading about what somebody else does. We ought to take another trip."

" We haven't been back from Florida very long," said Robert. " I don't think we ought to take another trip now. We all have our work to do on the farm, and we can't do it if we're always running off on pleasure trips. It wouldn't be fair to Mr. Bean. He feeds us and takes care of us, and we mustn't go back on him."

" That's right," said Freddy. " But I tell you what. I have an idea. Just wait till I run into my study for a minute. There's something I want to read to you."

Freddy had gathered together quite a library of old newspapers and printed advertising folders, which he kept in one corner of the pig-pen. He also had *The Complete Works of Shakespeare in One Volume,* which for many years had been almost indispensable to Mr. and Mrs. Bean, since they had used it to prop up the corner of their bed that didn't have any leg on it. But when they could afford it, they bought a new bed, and then the book was thrown out and Freddy got it.

Freddy was very proud of his study, although it was so dark in the pig-pen that nobody could possibly study there, or even read. But he knew all the different papers and pamphlets by their smell (the smell of *The Complete Works of Shakespeare in One Volume* differs from that of last week's newspaper more than you would believe), and so when he wanted to read anything, he just went in and got it and carried it outside.

Pretty soon he came back with a little booklet. On the cover it said: *Personally Conducted Tours to Europe.* And inside were pictures of some of the places people could be personally conducted to. Freddy read it aloud to them and explained how for a certain amount of money a person could join one of these tours, and then he didn't have to bother about buying his tickets or checking his baggage or anything. The company who ran the tour saw to everything, and it took him and all the other tourists round and showed them all the sights and got them back home safely. " And," said Freddy, " I don't see why we couldn't run such a company ourselves. Since we got back from Florida, lots of other animals, not only on this farm, but on other farms round here, have been wanting to take such a trip."

"I know a lot of mice that would like to go," said Eeny. "Only it's such a long way!"

"Oh, for animals that don't want to go far or can't get away for more than a day or two, we could get up short trips round here," said Freddy. "There are lots of interesting sights to see within just a short distance. Of course different animals are interested in different things. But we could have a tour of the ponds and rivers for ducks and geese, and a two-day trip to the cheese-factory for mice, and so on."

"I choose to personally conduct the mouse tour," said Jinx, with a laugh.

Eeny frowned. Being a mouse, he didn't have any eyebrows, and so he had to do most of it with his ears, which made him look quite terrifying, even though he was so small. It quite terrified Freddy.

" Please, Eeny, don't do that! " he exclaimed. " I'm sure Jinx didn't mean anything. You didn't, did you, Jinx? "

" No, no, certainly not," replied the cat. " Don't be so touchy, Eeny."

" You'd be touchy if your father and six aunts and fourteen uncles and nine brothers and sisters had been eaten by cats."

" Give you my word," said Jinx solemnly, " I haven't eaten a mouse in over a year. — Worse luck! " he added under his breath.

" What did you say? " asked Eeny suspiciously.

" Nothing," said Jinx, " nothing. Just purring because I'm glad you mice don't hate me any more."

" H'm," said Eeny scornfully, and was about to make a sharp retort, but Robert said: " Come on, stop your quarrelling. I think that's a great idea of yours, Freddy. But I've got to go now; I just heard a buggy stop at the gate and I must go bark at it so Mr. Bean will know he's got company. Let's

14

call a meeting in the cow-barn tonight and talk it over."

" Right," said the pig. " And then we'll form a company and incorporate."

" Incorporate? " asked Robert. " What's that? "

" Oh, I ran across it in reading," said Freddy importantly. " It's what all companies do. You draw up rules and by-laws and then you pay the government a fee, and then you're incorporated. That means that whatever you do after that is legal."

" Then we ought to do it," said Robert. " Good-bye, you animals. See you later."

CHAPTER II
BARNYARD TOURS, INC.

So THAT was how they started Barnyard
Tours, Inc. The " Inc." stands for " Incorporated." Freddy was president, and Jinx was
secretary, and Mrs. Wiggins was treasurer.
Mrs. Wiggins was the cow who lived in the
shed with Mrs. Wurzburger and Mrs. Wogus,
her two sisters, and Mrs. Wogus's little girl,
Marietta. Mrs. Wogus called Marietta her
little girl, but of course she was a calf. Mrs.
Wiggins was chosen treasurer because the
cow-shed made such a good treasury for the
various things that the tourist animals paid
the company. They brought all sorts of things,

16

but mostly things to eat, because these were what the company wanted most. This was a very good arrangement for Mr. Bean, because by and by he didn't have to feed the animals on the farm at all, and yet they were getting fat on the delicacies the tourists brought to them.

The tours started in a very small way, of course. The first one was for mice. Mrs. Wiggins took thirty mice on her back and went down the river road for a mile or two and then crossed the canal and came back the other way, stopping at the cheese-factory for lunch. The mice sat two by two, as you do in a sightseeing bus, and Eeny stood up in front, between Mrs. Wiggins's horns, and told them about the various points of interest they were passing, and pointed out bits of especially beautiful scenery and gave the names of the mice that lived in some of the finer residences. He was rather nervous at first, because he had never done any public speaking before, but after a while he began to enjoy it and grew quite poetic in the descriptive bits. Only he had to be careful not to make any jokes, because when he did, Mrs. Wiggins laughed heartily, and when she laughed, she shook so that the mice bounced about on her back, and once six of them fell off.

The mice were very much pleased with their trip and told all their friends, and gradually more and more animals came to the farm to inquire about tours. So many came finally that Mr. Bean was quite put out about it; he said he was sick and tired of seeing the barnyard crowded with strange animals, and he couldn't step foot outside the door without tripping over woodchucks and squirrels and rats or being bumped into by cows and horses. One night six skunks came, a father and mother and four children. One of the children wasn't very well, and they wanted to inquire about a place in the mountains to spend the summer where the water would be good and where the air would be bracing. The little skunks weren't very well brought up, and while the father and mother were in the barn talking to Jinx, they got to fighting, and they made so much noise that they waked up Mrs. Bean. She looked out the window and saw them, and of course she didn't know they had come on business, so she threw a pitcher of water on them. The mother skunk was quite mad, because she said the children might have caught their deaths of cold, being all wet through like that. Fortunately none of them took cold. But after that Robert said he thought they ought to open a regular office somewhere away from the house and near the road, where one animal could always be on hand to answer questions and give out information. Then they wouldn't bother Mr. and Mrs. Bean.

So they opened an office in an old shed that stood down in the corner of one of the fields quite a long way from the house. Most of the time Charles, the rooster, stayed in the office, because he was a very good talker, and he liked to tell other birds and animals things they didn't know. He was a good salesman. That means that he could often persuade animals to take trips that they really didn't care about taking at all. One time he talked so enthusiastically about the beautiful view you could get from the ten-acre lot, which was behind the house, on the hill, that he persuaded three horses from over near Centerboro to come up and plough it, just so they could see the view when they turned round at the end of each furrow. Mr. Bean was very much pleased when he found the field all ploughed.

After a number of short one-day trips had been carried out successfully, they began to get up longer ones. Jinx took a mixed party of cats and rabbits and cows on a ten-day tour of the Adirondacks. He looked up all the routes beforehand on a map that was in Freddy's library. They had a fine time — climbed mountains and went swimming and were royally entertained by the woods animals they met.

Special trips were arranged too for each kind of animal. The smaller animals particularly, who never dared venture alone very far from home, were very glad to see something of the world under the protection of such a brave and loyal dog as Robert, or such a reckless swashbuckler as Jinx. Freddy even got up a trip for spiders from the barn and the house and they all worked together in the morning and built a big web and then spent a glorious afternoon catching flies, and came home, very tired but very happy, early in the evening. In return they wove a big mosquito-net for Freddy to sleep under in the pig-pen. Of course it wasn't very strong and tore quite easily, but they agreed to keep it in repair for a year.

The hardest animals to get up trips for were cows. Cows aren't much interested in what is going on in the world. " It's hot and dusty out on the road," they said, " and dogs chase us, and automobiles make us hurry in a very undignified way. We'd rather stand round in the shade and swish our tails and think."

" But if you take a trip and see strange sights, you'll have more interesting things to think about," Freddy objected. Of course he knew as well as you do that it is almost impossible to catch a cow thinking. They have very good brains and they can think when they want to, but usually it's just too much trouble. They said that simply because they felt they ought to have *some* excuse for not ever doing anything. But Freddy went round and made a lot of inquiries and finally found several places that would interest cows. One place was a meadow on an abandoned farm that had very thick sweet grass, and another had historic interest for cows because over a hundred years ago a very famous cow had fought and killed a bear there, and another was a specially good place for them to stand in and switch their tails and think. But it took so much talking to persuade any cows to take the trip that although several parties were got up, Freddy decided it didn't pay. " The overhead is too high," Freddy said.

One day Freddy and Jinx were sitting inside the shed. It was a very hot day and they had talked for a while, and then Jinx had curled up and gone to sleep, and Freddy had started to look at a map of the arctic regions that a dog whose master kept a magazine stand had brought in and exchanged for a personally conducted tour through Scenic Centerboro. This was a very popular trip with dogs and cats, and would have been with other animals too, but the company didn't like to have its animal sightseers become too conspicuous. And so, of course, they couldn't go into towns and cities much. If people saw a party of dogs admiring the Centerboro Public Library — which was really very beautiful, built in the Gothic style — they wouldn't pay much attention to them. But if a party of rabbits or squirrels did the same thing, children would throw stones, and people would try to catch them, or at least would stare and make remarks, and it would be very unpleasant. And that would be bad for the company, because other animals would hear about it and wouldn't want to go on the tours.

While Freddy was poring sleepily over the map inside the shed, Charles, the rooster, was sitting on the fence outside, watching for customers. Charles liked the sound of his own voice pretty well, and when there wasn't anybody round to listen, he sometimes talked to himself. " Dear me," he was saying, " it *is* hot. Yes indeed, very hot. I do hope we'll get a shower to lay the dust." He kept saying this over and over. He was very economical and never wasted his best conversation on himself. Sometimes of course he said quite a good thing by mistake, but then he would save it up until someone came along and repeat it as if he had just thought of it.

By and by he saw something moving away off down the empty road. It got larger and larger, and pretty soon he saw it was a big grey farm horse. " Good gracious! " said Charles. " I wonder who that is. He walks very slowly, as if he were tired. He must have come a long way. Maybe he wants to take a tour.

" Good afternoon, horse," he said pleasantly when the animal had come near enough. " You a stranger in these parts? "

The horse did not answer, but came clumping stolidly along until he was opposite the shed.

Charles was naturally a little put out at being snubbed by a horse and he jumped down from the fence and walked out into the road. The horse saw him and stopped. " Excuse me, friend," he said. " Can you tell me if this is the place where there's a company that arranges trips for animals? "

" This is the place," said Charles, " and I'm part of the company. What can I do for you? We plan your vacations for you, tell you what to see and how to see it, conduct you to all points of greatest int — "

The horse shook his head slowly. " Ain't heard a word," he interrupted. " I know you're talkin' 'cause I can see your beak move,

"This is the place," said Charles, "and I'm part of the company."

but I ain't as young as I was, and I'm gettin' a little deef. Just hop up on my back like a good feller, and then we can talk comfortable."

As soon as Charles realized that the horse hadn't heard his first greeting and wasn't trying to snub him at all, he felt more agreeable, and he did as the other requested and repeated his remarks at greater length. But the horse still seemed doubtful.

" I understood there was a pig was president of this concern," he said. " I'd like to see him, I guess."

Charles glanced at the shed, from which came the mingled snores of one pig and one cat. " Our president is in conference just at present," he said importantly. " I'm afraid you couldn't see him without an appointment. But I am authorized to act for the company in these matters. If you tell me where you wish to go — "

" H'm," said the horse. " Well, I ain't ever got much information out of any rooster before — nor any information, for the matter of that, except maybe about what a smart feller he was, but maybe you're different. Anyway, I come a long way, and I don't want to go back empty-hoofed, so to speak. Ye see, I'm just a plain farm worker — have been all my life. I've worked hard. Now I'm gettin' old and I can't work like I used to, but while I still got some of my faculties, I'd like to see a little of the world. That's reasonable, ain't it? "

" Very commendable," said Charles.

" And so here I am. Now what kind of trips have you got? "

" Well, from what you say, I suppose you want a long trip, and the only long trip we're planning just now is one to Florida this winter. Our president is going to take this party himself. He's a seasoned traveller and has had a great deal of experience in conducting tours, and he knows everything there is to know about Florida. Of course it is a long trip and therefore rather more expensive than some of the — "

"That's what I wanted to talk to you about," interrupted the horse. "I'm poor. I haven't got anything to pay for the trip with."

"Oh, surely we can arrange that," said Charles. "Our charges are not excessive. A small bag of oats, or a bale of hay — "

"The farmer where I live is poor, too," the horse replied. "And as I don't do as much work as I used to, I don't get any more oats and hay than just barely enough to get along on. I can't save any of it. But I thought maybe I could work it out. I'd be willing to come over either before or after the trip and do, say, ten good days' work. I'm still strong and hearty. I wouldn't skimp ye on my part of the bargain."

"Dear me," said Charles, "that's very awkward — very awkward indeed. No, I'm very sorry, but I'm afraid that wouldn't do. It wouldn't do at all. Our rules are very strict, and our terms are strictly cash in advance."

" Ah," said the horse thoughtfully. " Well, I guess that finishes it, then. I thought maybe we could strike a bargain. But if that's the case — "

" I'm sorry," said Charles firmly. " But we have to be business-like, or where would we be? There's nothing personal in it, you understand — "

" Oh sure, I understand," said the horse impatiently. " Hop down now, I've got a long way to travel before night. Good day to ye. That's what I get for talking to a rooster, anyway." And he clumped off down the road.

Charles resumed his perch on the fence. " Stupid animal! " he said to himself. " Who ever heard of such a thing! Just like all of 'em: trying to get something for nothing. Oh, this being in business is not so easy. It takes lots of cleverness and tact and ability. It's a lucky day for the company when they got me to interview these animals. Why, suppose Freddy had been out here. For all his clever-

30

ness, he's not such a fine business man. Just between you and me, Charles, you handled that horse pretty well."

The longer Charles thought about it, the more pleased with himself he became, and finally he got so puffed up with pride that he went in and waked Freddy up and told him about it. But, to his amazement, Freddy was not at all pleased.

" What! " he exclaimed, " he offered to work his way on the trip, and you sent him away? Why, you ninny, that's the best idea I've heard since the company started. Why, you miserable fowl you, you oaf, you — you *umph!* "

" Umph " is a word that pigs use only when they are thoroughly disgusted with people. If a pig calls you an umph, you have a right to get mad about it — unless, of course, you happen to be one. Charles ruffled up the feathers in his neck and started to get mad, but before he could think of anything sarcastic to say, Freddy pushed him aside, crawled through the fence, and trotted off up the road in the direction the horse had taken.

Jinx hadn't waked up, and Charles tiptoed out of the shed, and walked dejectedly back to his home in the hen-coop. " That's gratitude for you! " he muttered. " Work and slave for these animals day in and day out, and what thanks do I get? Get called an umph. An umph — me! Well, I'm through, that's all. They can get somebody else to interview the tourists. We'll see how many they get when I'm not round."

But the next morning when Mrs. Wiggins told him that there was to be a meeting of the company at ten o'clock, his curiosity was too much for him, and he got to the office before anybody but Freddy had come. Freddy was again looking over the map of the arctic regions. Charles, whose feelings were still hurt, would have gone out, but Freddy said:

" Don't go, Charles. I'm sorry I was rude to you yesterday. Please forgive me, will you? "

Of course there was nothing for Charles to do but to accept the apology, which he did, very handsomely. " Certainly, Freddy," he said. " Pray don't mention it again." He was going on to say more, because no matter how long he had talked, he could always find more to say on any subject, and he had hardly said anything yet, but the other animals began to arrive, and pretty soon Freddy called the meeting to order.

" Ladies and gentlemen, friends and fellow stockholders," he said, " I have the great pleasure to announce to you that at the end of the first three months of business, your company finds itself in a very strong position. Although no very long trips have been organized, twenty-eight short trips have been successfully completed without loss or damage to any client, with the exception of one spider, who lost three legs on the third Fly-catching Expedition in a fight with a wasp, and one mouse who had indigestion as a result of eating too much cheese at the cheese-factory on Scenic Tour No. 3 for Mice. Both of these unfortunates, I am happy to say, have stated of their own free will that the company is not to blame. In addition to such profits of the business as have already been divided up, there is in the treasury a substantial surplus of nuts, grain, and various kinds of food, as well as of odds and ends which we have accepted in payment, and which we shall undoubtedly find use for later."

There were loud cheers at this very favourable report, and then Freddy went on:

" But the principal reason for calling this meeting is that something happened which showed me a new way in which the company can benefit both us and our friend and owner, Mr. Bean."

" Three cheers for Mr. Bean," called Hank, the old white horse, and the animals cheered lustily, for Mr. Bean was well liked. Even Mr. and Mrs. Webb, the spiders, who had come to the meeting on Mrs. Wiggins's back, cheered heartily, but of course nobody heard them.

Then Freddy told them about the horse. " He wants to take a long trip, but he hasn't anything to pay for it with, so he has offered to give two weeks' work. Do you see what that means, animals? That means that Hank, here, can take two weeks' vacation whenever he wants to. Now, suppose for every animal, bird, and insect here we can get a substitute in this way. Two weeks' vacation for us all. And there is no need to limit it to two weeks. Up to today there has been one great difficulty in getting up tours. Most animals haven't anything to pay with. But there are hundreds who will be willing to work their way. I see no reason why Mr. Bean should not have twice as many animals at work on the farm as he has now. And at the same time I see no reason why any of us should ever have to work again."

At this there was a perfectly tremendous burst of cheering, and then all the animals came up and shook hands with Freddy and congratulated him on having such a fine idea. Mrs. Wiggins was so enthusiastic that she slapped him on the back, and as she was a large cow and Freddy was a rather small pig, she knocked him clean through the side of the shed. He took two boards out with him as he went and this weakened the shed so that the roof fell right down on top of the meeting. But nobody was hurt, and all the animals scrambled out except Mrs. Wiggins who was so ashamed of what she had done that she just stayed right there until they got worried about her and pulled her out. And then when she saw Freddy's black eye, and the awful damage she had done to the office of the company, she broke down and cried and wanted to go home, and it was quite a long time before Freddy could comfort her and persuade her that nobody thought it was her fault.

The animals went to work on the new scheme right away. It was really quite a good scheme. You see, on a farm every bird and animal gets food and lodging from the farmer. In return he is supposed to do certain work. A horse's duty is to draw ploughs and wagons and buggies; and a dog's duty is to bark at strangers and do tricks and keep an eye on the children and look intelligent when his master talks to him; and a cat's duty is to chase mice, and purr when he's petted and sleep in ladies' laps and sit on the fence nights and sing. Some animals don't have any special duties. A pig's duty is just to be a pig, which isn't very hard if you have a good appetite.

Most of the work is done in the summer, and that is why it was so easy for the animals to get off and go to Florida as they had the previous winter. But now, if they could get substitutes, it would be easy for them to get off at any time of the year. So they went round and saw all the animals on the near-by farms and told them about the new scheme. And they found cows and horses and sheep and pigs and goats and cats and dogs — ninety-four animals in all, not counting birds and insects and wild animals like chipmunks and skunks and rabbits — who each agreed to do two weeks' work the following summer if they could be taken on the Florida trip. For the next two months Barnyard Tours, Inc., was a pretty busy company. Hundreds of animals who had never before been able to afford even the short sightseeing trips came to the farm and offered one or two hours' work if they could take a one- or two-day tour. Freddy and Jinx and Robert and Charles and Hank and even Mrs. Wiggins were almost never home. They were off every day personally conducting groups of animal tourists. The mice — Eek and Quik and Eeny and Cousin Augustus — took so many parties of rats and mice and chipmunks to the cheese-factory that they began to get very fat, and they had to have all the mouse holes in the barn enlarged so they could get through them. Of course they got the tourists to do all the heavy gnawing.

Mr. Bean was delighted with the way the work on the farm was getting done. The day he ploughed the twenty-acre field, thirty-five horses came and helped him, and it didn't take more than half an hour. Then one day he started to paint the barn. He painted one side of it before supper, and he was going to paint the rest the next day. But that night Freddy got a lot of squirrels down from the woods, and they finished the job before morning. They dipped their tails in the paint and used them as brushes, and then, when they were through, they cleaned them off with turpentine. There wasn't enough turpentine, and three of the squirrels had to go round with white tails all the following winter, till the paint wore off.

One evening Jinx heard Mr. Bean say to his wife: " Mrs. B., if the stumps were cleared out of that lot down back of the pond and it was planted with potatoes next year, we'd make a lot of money."

" You've often said, Mr. B.," replied his wife, " that there was money to be made out of that lot. Many and many's the time I've

39

heard you say it. But it would take an awful lot of work."

"Yes," said Mr. Bean, "And I'm not as young as I was. Not by a whole lot, I ain't. And I've come to the time of life when I want to sit back and not work so hard. We've got plenty to get along on. What's the use making more money when we ain't got any children to leave it to? I guess we'll leave them stumps alone." And he leaned back and puffed hard on his pipe, and the smoke trickled out of his bushy whiskers so that he looked like a haystack about to burst into flames.

And Mrs. Bean sighed and said: "This is a nice farm. But it's lonesome for just us two. I do wish we had some children to leave it to."

But Jinx jumped up and ran out into the barn and called a meeting, and the next night nearly two hundred animals gathered down in the lot beyond the pond and set to work to clean out the stumps. They went at it with paws and claws and snouts — dogs and pigs and woodchucks and squirrels and rabbits and even mice — and the dirt simply flew out of the holes. Then when they had dug all around one stump, and the roots had been gnawed through, the horses would put a rope around it and pull it down to the end of the field. By morning there wasn't a stump left and when Mr. Bean leaned out of his window just after sunrise to see what kind of day it was going to be, he noticed a big pile of stumps away down across the pond that hadn't been there the night before. At first he didn't know what had happened, but when he had got out his telescope and had a good look, he hurried into his clothes and hurried downstairs and " Hurry up my breakfast, Mrs. B.," he called. " There's queer goings-on on this farm, and I've got to find out about 'em." But he didn't take time for much breakfast. He ate only three eggs and four sausages and two stacks of buckwheat cakes and a cup of coffee and five slices of toast, and then he hurried to the lot beyond the pond. And when he saw that the stumps were all cleaned out and piled up neatly in a corner of the lot, he stared and stared. And then he said very slowly two or three times: " Peter grieve us! " And then he went back to the house and told Mrs. Bean.

" All we've got to do now is plough that field and plant it next spring," he said. " Bushels and bushels of potatoes just for a little work. I want to tell you, Mrs. B.," he said, " that hereafter these animals can do what they please around here. I've farmed this place, man and boy, for fifty-two years, but those animals are better farmers than I am."

Mrs. Bean looked at him in surprise. " I never thought I'd live to see the day, Mr. B., when you'd admit that any human being, let alone an animal, knew more about farming than you did. And, whatever you say, I'll never believe it. But I think the least thing we can do, Mr. B., is to give the animals a party."

CHAPTER III
THE EXPLORERS SET OUT

Now there isn't room to tell about the party the Beans gave, nor how they invited all the animals and people for miles around, nor of the eating and drinking and dancing and merrymaking, nor of how the barns and pens and coops were illuminated with coloured lights, and fireworks were set off, and everybody had a perfectly grand time and didn't get home until after midnight. A little while after, the ninety-four tourist animals started off for Florida. They divided into four parties, and Freddy and Jinx and Robert and Hank were each put in charge of one party. The trip was a complete success in every way. When they came back in the spring, Hank's party brought back a wagon load of coconuts, which Mr. Bean sold to his neighbours for ten cents apiece, and Freddy's party brought back a lot of very handsome picture postcards of all the places they had visited, which Mrs. Bean was much pleased with and tacked up on the wall in the sitting-room. The others didn't bring anything, but two young alligators, named Armando and Juanita, came back with Robert. He had rescued them from a man who had caught them in the Everglades and was taking them to be sold into captivity. They were very grateful to Robert and cried so bitterly when they heard he was going back home and wasn't going to take them along that he decided to let them come. They followed him about everywhere. " Just like dogs," said Mrs. Wiggins, and shook with laughter at the thought of a faithful pet like Robert having faithful pets of his own.

All that spring Barnyard Tours, Inc., was

very busy. The roads were so full of travelling animals that automobile traffic was seriously interfered with and the Rome and Utica and Syracuse automobile clubs complained to the Mayor of Centerboro, and the Mayor of Centerboro called up Mr. Bean on the telephone and said that something would have to be done. Mr. Bean promised to do something, but before he could decide what to do, Freddy saw an editorial complaining about it in the Centerboro paper, and he told the other animals. So they were more careful after that and took back roads or went cross-country whenever possible.

The work on the farm was done as if by magic. Whatever Mr. Bean said he was going to do got done before he had time to do it. If he said in the evening: " Tomorrow I'm going to plough the lower pasture," in the morning when he went out to plough it, the work would all be done. Even most of Mrs. Bean's work was done for her by the animals. At first when she came into the kitchen and found a dozen squirrels busily sweeping the floor with their tails, she shooed them out quickly. But after she found out that they were helping her, she let them alone. She would sit comfortably in her rocking-chair and doze while dozens of little animals ran all over the house, picking up and dusting and sweeping. Now and then she would smile and lean down and pat a mouse on the head who was hurrying out with a mouthful of threads he had picked off the floor, and now and then one of the squirrels or rabbits or cats would jump up in her lap to have his head scratched. Of course the animals couldn't cook and sew and make beds, but they were a great help and they kept the house as neat as a pin.

But Freddy and Jinx and the other members of the firm were growing restless. They had no regular work to do on the farm any more, for with so many animals paying for trips with work, there were more workers than work to be done. And after they had personally conducted tour after tour over the same ground, they began to get tired of it.

"Personally," said Freddy, "I'm fed up. I'm sick to death of that Scenic Centerboro tour, of explaining over and over again to groups of silly animals about the Public Library and the Presbyterian Church and the fine view from the hill behind the Trumbull place. And the foolish questions they ask! And the complaints!"

"You said a snoutful, pig," said Jinx, who was inclined to be a little vulgar in his speech, but was otherwise a very estimable animal. "And the smaller they are, the more complaints they have. A cow or a horse, now, will take things good-naturedly and won't expect too much. But there were a couple of beetles on that last trip — my word, but they were unpleasant people! I carried 'em all the way on my back, and first they couldn't see, and then the dust got in their noses, and then when it began to rain and there wasn't any more dust, they complained about that and tried to crawl into my ears to get out of the wet. Can you beat that? "

" We don't have to beat it," said Freddy seriously. Freddy had become very serious during the past year, and rather dignified. Once he had been a carefree, light-hearted young pig, always playing jokes or writing poetry or inventing new games, but the cares of business had weighed him down, and nowadays he almost never even smiled. Which was too bad, since a pig's face is built for smiling, and Freddy never looked so handsome as when he was squealing with laughter. " You see," he went on, " I've been figuring up and we've got enough work coming to us for the trips we've been taking animals on so that we could all go away for two years if we wanted to, and all the farm work would be done while we were away. We don't have to have any more trips for two years. Now I've got a plan. What do you say we go find the north pole? "

Jinx didn't want to let on that he had never heard of the north pole, so he just said:

" Fine! That's a great idea, Freddy. How do we get there? "

So Freddy explained that the north pole was at the top of the world — that if you went straight north, you'd reach it, and that if you kept right on going in the same direction after you had passed the pole, you'd be going south again. Jinx didn't understand this very well; in fact, he didn't really believe it at all; but he was so tired of the life he had been leading for the past few months that he didn't care much what he did as long as it was something different. And so he was very enthusiastic about it and went with Freddy down to the study, where they got out maps and spent the whole afternoon laying out routes and deciding whom they would ask to go with them.

For this wasn't a trip that just any animal could go on. " We want only hard seasoned travellers," said Freddy, " animals who can put up with danger and hardship, who are willing to be cold and uncomfortable and hungry and weary for days on end. This won't be like going to Florida. But who wants to go to Florida? — a soft trip like that! This will be a real adventure. And if we make it, think of the honour of being the first animals to visit the north pole! Why, I bet we get our pictures in the New York papers! "

This was enough for Jinx. He was rather vain of his good looks, and thought how fine it would be to see his picture on the front page of all the papers and to have hundreds of people all over the country saying: " Look! Look! Here's that wonderful cat that went to the north pole! Isn't he a beauty? " But all he said was: " Well, when do we start? "

" No reason to wait," said Freddy. " We'll go talk to the others right now." And by bed-time Robert, the dog, and Hank, the old white horse, and Mrs. Wogus, who was Mrs. Wiggins's sister, and Ferdinand, the sarcastic old crow, had all agreed to go. Some of the other animals they asked refused. Mrs. Wiggins said no, she was too old and she liked her comfort too much to go traipsing off into the wilds.

Charles, the rooster, wanted very much to go, but his wife Henrietta wouldn't hear of it. The general feeling in the barnyard seemed to be that it was very foolish to leave comfortable homes to explore a country that consisted of nothing but snow and ice, that was certainly uncomfortable and probably dangerous.

But none of these sensible arguments could persuade the six adventurers, who, like all the brave spirits who have made history and sailed unknown seas and charted unknown continents in the past, cared less for ease than for glory and laughed at danger and hardship.

And so on a bright morning a week later they set out on their perilous journey. First came Hank, the old white horse, harnessed to the rickety phaeton that they had brought back from their trip to Florida. Inside the phaeton rode Freddy and Jinx, but there wasn't much room even for them, for most of the space was taken up with piles of cast-off blankets and old overcoats which they had gathered, with the help of their friends, from all the neighbouring farms and with which they planned to keep warm in the polar regions. Behind the phaeton walked Mrs. Wogus, and when it went up a hill, she helped Hank by putting her forehead against the back of the vehicle and pushing. Robert ran alongside, and Ferdinand, who had rather a sour disposition, sat on the dash-board, with his eyes shut, looking very bored and weary, as they drove out of the yard.

The Beans, of course, knew nothing about the trip, but when they heard the commotion outside, they jumped up from their breakfast and ran out on the porch.

" Why, I do believe," said Mrs. Bean, " that they're starting out on another trip! Well, well, will wonders never cease? "

" So they are, Mrs. B.," replied her husband. " Now I wonder where they're off to this time. Consarn it, I wish we could talk animal talk; then we'd know. But hey, Hank! " he called. " Wait a minute! Whoa! Back up there! " And as Hank stopped obediently,

Mr. Bean dashed into the house and presently returned with his second-best night-cap, a white one with a red tassel, which he tied to the top of the phaeton. " There," he said, " now you've got a flag. Good-bye, animals! Have a good time, and remember there's a good home and a warm welcome waiting for you when you get tired of the road."

" Good-bye! " called Mrs. Bean. " Be careful about automobiles and don't sit in draughts or get under trees in thunder-storms or stay up too late nights or — " But the rest of her advice was drowned in the cheers of the animals who were staying behind, as the little procession marched out of the gate, with the standard of the house of Bean waving above them.

But, for all the cheering and waving of paws and claws and hoofs and handkerchiefs, Ferdinand, perched on the dash-board, never even opened his eyes.

CHAPTER IV
FERDINAND RETURNS

LIFE on the farm went along quietly all that summer. As the fame of Barnyard Tours, Inc., increased, more and more animals kept coming to inquire about trips, and Charles, the rooster, was kept very busy in the office from early morning till late at night, answering questions and making up parties. After the first week nothing was heard of the explorers until fall, when the birds began to fly past on their way south for the winter. Then an occasional woodpecker or white-throat would swoop down into the big elm and deliver a message. The animals learned that everything was going well; that Freddy had had a bad

54

cold, but was better; that Ferdinand had had a fight with a gang of thieving blue jays and had beaten them badly; that the expedition had high hopes of reaching the pole before Christmas, in which case they would be back home by midsummer.

The winter came and passed without more news. In the spring two chickadees who had been living in the elm since October announced that they were starting for the north, and agreed, in return for the grain and bits of suet with which Charles had fed them all winter, to come back if they learned anything of the wanderers and give their report before going ahead with the house that they planned to build that spring in Labrador. But the chickadees did not come back. They might, of course, have been caught and eaten by hawks or cats. They might have decided that it was too far to come all the way back to the farm, just to tell the animals that their friends were well. But still they hadn't come back, and the animals worried. Every day Charles sent one of his eight daughters, who were growing up now into long-legged noisy chickens, with manners that were the despair of Henrietta, their mother, to perch on the gatepost and watch the road for the first sign of the returning travellers. But July passed, August passed, and no one came.

And then at last the animals decided that something must be done. It was Mrs. Wiggins who really got things going. " I just can't sleep nights," she complained, " for thinking of those dear friends away off up there in the cold and the snow, maybe without anything to eat, and my own dear sister, Mrs. Wogus, with them; and her little girl, Marietta, sobbing herself to sleep every night because she wants her mother back. We've got to do something, and we're *going* to do something. Even if I have to go alone, I'm going to start out and find them. If anyone else wants to come along, he can, but I'm going anyway."

" A very laudable resolve, Mrs. Wiggins," said Charles. " A very brave and noble resolution. I've been thinking myself for some time that a rescue party should be formed."

" Then why didn't you say something about it? " Mrs. Wiggins demanded. She knew perfectly well that the idea had never occurred to the rooster.

" I thought it best to wait," replied Charles with dignity, " until we were really sure that something hadn't gone wrong. We'd look rather foolish starting out to rescue them and then meeting them half a mile down the road, wouldn't we? "

" There are some things worse than looking foolish," snapped Mrs. Wiggins, " though no selfish, stuck-up rooster would ever know it."

" I take no offence at your words," said Charles, " since I realize the anxiety that you must be feeling, and that, after all, I share with you. Certainly, though, you won't be permitted to go on this quest alone. I'm sure that every animal in the barnyard will want to take part. Personally — "

57

"They can do as they please," Mrs. Wiggins interrupted. "I start tomorrow morning." And she turned her back on Charles and went on moodily chewing her cud.

But the next morning when she came out of the cow-shed, firm in her resolve to start for the north without delay, she was surprised to find a great crowd of animals of all kinds waiting for her. The afternoon before, Charles had sent his eight daughters and his seven sons round to all the farms in the neighbourhood to call for volunteers for the rescue party, and as all the adventurers except Ferdinand were very popular, nearly every animal who could get away had agreed to go. There they were, waiting, and as Mrs. Wiggins came out they gave a cheer that brought the night-capped heads of Mr. and Mrs. Bean to the window.

"What's all this?" asked Mrs. Wiggins as the animals crowded around her.

Charles stepped forward and explained. "Of course," he said, "we can't all go, for there are nearly a hundred of us volunteers

58

"What's all this?" asked Mrs. Wiggins

here, and the rescue party shouldn't consist of more than ten or fifteen. Some of us, therefore, will have to resign the privilege of engaging in this glorious venture and remain at home, disappointed, but happy in the knowledge that in volunteering we have done our manifest duty. In order to avoid the embarrassment which any of you may feel in dropping out now," he went on, turning to the crowd of animals, " I will set the example by voluntarily withdrawing from the rescue party. Much as my heart has been set on it, eagerly as I have looked forward to this venture, I shall yet be able with dry eyes to watch the departure of the devoted band among whom I had hoped to number myself, since I shall — "

But the speech was never finished, for with an angry clucking Henrietta, his wife, pushed her way through the circle of curious animals. " What's all this I hear? " she demanded. " Not going, did you say? Well, just let me see you try to stay at home! You'll wish you'd never been hatched, that's all I've got to say! To desert your friends when they're in want and danger — I never heard such cowardly nonsense! You're going, and, what's more, I'm going with you, to see there's no shirking."

" Tut, tut, my dear," said Charles in a whisper. " You don't understand. Of course I'm going. But all these animals can't go, and I was merely — "

But Henrietta cuffed him aside with her wing. " You be quiet, young man, if you know what's good for you. — And now, Mrs. Wiggins," she went on, " I take it what you want is to get started as soon as possible. If we let my husband do any more talking, we shan't get started for a week. What I suggest is that you select the animals you want to have with you on this trip yourself. Isn't that fair, animals? "

They all agreed and formed a long line, which went twice around the barnyard and out into the road, and Mrs. Wiggins walked up and down and tried to make her choice, but all the animals wanted to go so badly that she didn't have the heart to dismiss any of them, and finally she got so mixed up and confused that she just sat down in the middle of the barnyard and cried.

Mrs. Wiggins didn't have much of an education, but she had a good heart, and all the animals were very fond of her, so they all crowded round to try to cheer her up. But there were so many of them that those on the outside of the crowd who couldn't get near her began to push, and then the ones they had pushed got angry and pushed back, and pretty soon the whole barnyard was a mob of angry animals, growling and pushing and shoving, and in the middle, almost smothered, was Mrs. Wiggins.

Goodness knows what might have happened if at that moment Charles's eldest daughter, Leah, whose turn it was to sit on the fence and watch the road, hadn't come dashing into the yard with the news that she thought she had seen Ferdinand away off up the road. At once all the animals disentangled themselves and rushed out the gate, and, sure enough, a quarter of a mile up the road they saw a small black figure coming slowly towards them. It limped, and one wing hung down and trailed in the dust, but it was certainly a crow, and as it came nearer, they saw that it was indeed Ferdinand.

The animals surrounded him and nearly deafened him with questions. Since he couldn't have been heard if he had tried to answer, he simply trudged along through the gate, across the yard, and into the barn, where he took a long drink from the watering-trough, then came outside and raised his claw for silence.

"My friends," he said when his audience had stopped whispering and shuffling and try-ing to edge themselves into a better position, "I have been on the road for nearly two months, walking all the time, for, as you see, my wing is broken. To tell you all that has happened is too long a story, for I have come back to get help, and we must start at once. But three months ago we had reached the Arctic Ocean. We had camped on the shore while Freddy worked out with his map the route we were to follow in our dash for the pole. Everything had gone well so far; we were very happy and comfortable in the tent we made with the blankets, and with few exceptions all the animals of the North had been very friendly and helpful. It was warmer that night than it had been in some time, and all around us we heard the ice cracking and booming as it split and melted. We thought we had camped far enough back from the shore to be safe, but in the morning when we stepped outside the tent door, there was water all around us. The piece of ice we had been camping on had split off during the night and we were on an iceberg in the middle of the Arctic Ocean."

A buzz of excitement went up from the animals and they crowded closer to listen. Mrs.

Wiggins was sobbing softly. " My poor sister," she gulped.

" You needn't be alarmed, madam," said Ferdinand impatiently. " Your sister is quite safe. Whether you will ever see her again, however, is another matter. To continue: we had plenty to eat, and our fur coats and the tent kept us warm. But as we drifted, day after day, the iceberg slowly melted and large chunks split off and fell into the water. It was only a matter of time when there would no longer be room for us all to stand on it. As the only member of the party who could fly, I had gone on a number of scouting expeditions to see if we could get help. But although a number of animals were willing to do anything they could, there was really nothing they could do. A school of whales came by one day, and they all put their heads against the berg and tried to push it towards land, but it was so slippery that they kept slipping off and bumping into one another, and finally they gave up.

65

" On one of my flights I had seen that we were approaching land, and I figured that we should pass within half a mile of it in about two days. We had decided that our only chance of escape was for the animals to try to swim that half-mile to shore. There was little hope of their reaching it, for even Freddy, who, as you know, is a champion swimmer and has won several prizes, could not hope to stay long afloat in that icy water. But there was no other way, and we had made up our minds to it, when on the very morning we had fixed for the attempt, on coming out of the ice cave in which we had been camping, we saw that a ship had come alongside the berg, and the sailors were climbing up its steep sides. They had seen the phaeton, which stood outside the cave on a ledge, and had come to find out how it got there.

" The sailors were greatly surprised to find a cow and a cat and a dog and a pig and a horse and a crow on an iceberg in the open sea, and they took us all on board and made

quite a fuss over us. They were particularly
delighted with Mrs. Wogus, for the only milk
they had had for the past six months had been
condensed milk out of a can. Just before we
all went aboard, Freddy took me aside. ' Don't
let them catch you, Ferdinand,' he said.
' These sailors won't let us go if they can help
it, but there's still hope while you're free.'
So I flew up on top of the berg where they
couldn't reach me. I stayed round for two
days, and I must say those sailors treated the
animals like kings and queens. They took
turns riding Hank round the deck, and they
made leather collars for Jinx and Robert, and
they were so pleased with Mrs. Wogus that
they gave her a cabin all to herself with lace
curtains at the windows, and the captain took
off his hat to her whenever she came on deck.
They treated Freddy well, too, but I didn't
just like the greedy way some of them looked
at him, and once when Freddy went by, I saw
the mate nudge the captain in the ribs, and
heard him say: ' A nice dish of pig's knuckles

and sauerkraut now, eh, Mr. Hooker?'
And the captain said: 'Chops, Mr. Pomeroy; chops is my choice — with a bit of apple.' And they both licked their lips and
grinned.

"Well, that can't be helped, and what's
happened now, nobody knows. For my part,
I think they were just fooling and said those
things because they wanted to see Freddy get
pale. Pigs look so funny when they are scared.
But, to make a long story short, on the third
day Freddy said to me: ' You'd better go now.
I've found out that this ship is a whaling
ship, but they've had a bad year and haven't
caught a single whale, so they've decided to
take a vacation from whaling and see if they
can't find Santa Claus's house. You know he
lives up round the north pole somewhere.
They're going to sail north as far as they can,
and then when they get stuck in the ice, they'll
go on foot. You'd better fly home as fast as
you can and bring help for us.' Then he said
good-bye to me. ' You may never see me again,

68

Ferdinand,' he said mournfully. ' These sailors are nice and friendly to me, but they're big fat men, all pork-eaters — I can tell a pork-eater just by the way he looks at me, so greedy it makes me fairly blush sometimes — and what's friendship to a hungry man? ' ' Oh, cheer up,' I said. ' A little pig like you wouldn't make more'n a breakfast for the cabin boy. They'll try to fatten you up first, and if you're careful of your diet and watch the calories and keep off starchy foods, you'll stay thin, and I'll round up some of your friends and have them back here to rescue you before anything serious happens.' Well, that didn't seem to comfort him much, for Freddy likes to eat almost better than he likes to make up poetry, but we said good-bye and I started flying home. I'd have been here long before this, for I was flying day and night, if I hadn't run into a telegraph wire on the fourth night and broken my wing. It's mending all right and I'll be able to fly in another week, but meanwhile I've had to walk.

" And now I've talked enough. I call for volunteers to rescue our friends and neighbours from captivity in the Far North. Who'll go? "

CHAPTER V
THE RESCUE PARTY

OF COURSE all the animals wanted to go, but Ferdinand wouldn't stand for any nonsense, and he lined them up and very soon had picked five and dismissed the others. Those he had chosen grouped themselves round him, looking very important. There were Mrs. Wiggins, and Jack, the big black dog, and a wise old grey horse who lived over near Centerboro and had once been in a circus. He was Hank's uncle, and everybody called him Uncle William. And there was a porcupine named Cecil, who lived back in the woods and was very slow and lazy and rather stupid, but

71

Ferdinand thought he would be a good one to have along, since a porcupine can go anywhere and no other animal will molest him. And lastly there was a close friend of Ferdinand's, a wicked-looking billy-goat (his name really was Bill), whom none of the animals liked because he was so malicious and bad-tempered. The only nice thing about him was that he was so fond of Ferdinand. They used to spend hours together down in the far pasture, their heads together, and the other animals, hearing the crow's harsh laughter and the goat's wicked giggle, used to wonder what mischief they were hatching. But, whatever it was, none of them ever found out.

At Mrs. Wiggins's request, Charles and Henrietta were allowed to join the party, although Ferdinand grumbled that he didn't see what they wanted to take a lot of poultry along for. But when the four mice who had been on the first trip to Florida came boldly forward and said they were going too, he burst into harsh laughter. " Mice! " he exclaimed.

" Who ever heard of mice on an arctic expedition? What good could you do, I'd like to know? Could you fight a walrus or lick a polar bear? Listen to this, Bill. Look what wants to join the rescue party. Why, you can't hardly *see* 'em! "

Now nothing makes a mouse madder than to be made fun of on account of his size, and when Eek and Quik and Eeny and Cousin Augustus heard the loud laughter of Bill and Ferdinand and the suppressed snickers of the other animals, they were wild with rage. " What could we do, eh? " shouted Eeny, and his voice was about as loud as the whistle on a peanut stand. " We'll *show* you what! You big black imitation of a stuffed mantelpiece ornament! Come on, boys! " And with that he and Eek made a rush for the crow, while Quik and Cousin Augustus dashed at Bill and, swarming up his legs before he could shake them off, ran up along his back and began chewing at his ears. Ferdinand tried to hold off the mice by jabbing at them with his beak,

73

but they managed to keep behind him and dash in and nip his ankles whenever they saw an opening, until he cawed with pain. Meanwhile Bill was shaking his head and dancing and bucking frantically to get rid of the other two mice, but they just dug their sharp little teeth in deeper and hung on.

" Stop! " yelled Ferdinand. " Oh — ouch! Stop it, I say! I take it all back; you're worse'n lions and tigers. I'll let you go if you'll — ow *yow!* — if you'll only *quit!* "

So Eek and Eeny quit and sat down on the door-sill and didn't say anything at all, which was very sensible of them, because it is very silly, when you've won an argument, to keep on arguing. And the other two mice jumped off Bill's back and sat down beside them, and then Ferdinand made a speech. It was rather a good speech, but it was also rather too long, as most speeches are, so it is not set down here. He told the animals that he was going to be captain of the expedition, since he had had some arctic experience and knew what roads they would have to travel, and he said that any animal who wasn't willing to agree to take orders from him had better drop out right now at the start. He said that it was a long, hard, perilous trip they were starting on, as he knew personally, and that he expected every animal to do his duty. And when the speech was over, the mice climbed aboard Mrs. Wiggins, and Charles and Henrietta climbed aboard Uncle William, and Ferdinand perched on one of Bill's horns, and the party set out amid the prolonged cheering of the stay-at-homes.

For the first few days they travelled steadily northward through a pleasant farming country. The people here had become accustomed to seeing a great many animals on the roads and paid little attention to them. But as they got farther north, and the farms began to give way to woodland, the people were more curious about them, and they had one or two narrow escapes from being captured, so they did most of their travelling by night. They had a good deal of trouble with Cecil. Porcupines can't walk very fast, and Cecil was always lagging behind and making them wait for him. They tried having him ride on Uncle William's back, but they only tried it once, for his quills were as sharp as needles, and every time he moved, a dozen or so of them would stick into Uncle William. He was awfully sorry and apologetic about it, but, as Uncle William said, apologies make poor poultices. So after that Cecil walked again, and the others just had to put up with his slowness.

As they went on, the woods grew thicker and wilder, and the roads grew narrower and ruttier, and the houses fewer and farther between. By the end of the first week Ferdinand's wing was all right again, so that he could fly on ahead and spy out the land, and this enabled them to take a good many short cuts. One night they crossed the Saint Lawrence River by a long bridge, and then they were in Canada. They had some trouble crossing the bridge because customs men lie in wait at each end and make travellers pay a tax on certain articles. These articles that can't be brought into a country without paying are called dutiable. Of course the animals didn't have any luggage with them, but the Canadian customs man thought some of the animals themselves were dutiable, so he held them up. " Let's see," he said. " Milk and feathers and beef and hides — I dunno but there's a duty on all of 'em." And he took out a little book and licked his thumb and began looking through the pages to see if he could find out what the duty would be on Mrs. Wiggins and Charles and Henrietta. Things looked bad for a minute, but Ferdinand whispered in the goat's ear and then flew straight at the man and knocked the book out of his hand. The latter stooped to pick it up, and as he did so, Bill put his head down and charged at him. The goat's hard head with the strong curving horns hit the seat of the customs man's trousers with a smack and shot him into the ditch at the side of the road, and before he had even begun to pick himself up, the animals had galloped off into the night.

Soon after this the roads disappeared altogether and they plodded along through the deep forest. The woods animals were very kind to them and showed them paths and gave them directions how to avoid swamps and lakes. Sometimes a deer would guide them for a day or more over the forest trails, just for the sake of hearing a little gossip about what was going on in the outside world. Deer lead very secluded lives, and although they are curious, they are too timid ever to venture into the more cultivated regions where important things are going on. A quite small bit of gossip will last a deer for a month, and he'll tell it over and over to all his friends, and they hurry to tell it to their friends, until it is known all over the north country. But they are very honest animals and never gossip maliciously.

One afternoon the animals came out of the gloomy forest on to the shore of a shining lake.

At their feet — which were hot and dusty, for they had walked fast and far — a beach of fine white sand sloped down into the cool water. With a whoop they dashed down and were soon splashing and shouting and playing the kind of tricks on each other that are lots of fun when you play them on someone else, but not so funny when they're played on you. Even the mice found a little pool between two stones, about half an inch deep, where Eeny, who had taken lessons in swimming from Freddy, showed them how to swim the breast stroke. But of course mice never make good swimmers.

Mrs. Wiggins wasn't a very good swimmer either. She had practised a good deal in the pond at home, and maybe she would have learned, but she was so clumsy in the water and looked so frightened that the other animals all laughed at her, and then she would begin to laugh at herself and would swallow water and choke and have to be towed ashore practically helpless. Today she was just paddling round when Bill decided that it would be fun to duck her. He climbed up on her back in the water, and down she went. When she came up, she looked so bewildered that they all went into fits of laughter, and Bill did it again. Then he did it again. Then Mrs. Wiggins waded ashore and sat down in the sand. " I like a joke as well as the next one," she said, " but enough's enough."

The late afternoon sun wasn't very hot and she felt a little chilly, so she decided to take a walk along the shore to get warm. When she got down to the end of the beach, she went round a point, and there on the other side was another little beach, and behind it a tumbledown house in a clearing. Corn was growing in the clearing, and Mrs. Wiggins was very fond of corn. There were no people in sight, and the house looked deserted, but " It's better to be safe than sorry," said Mrs. Wiggins to herself, and so she crouched down and tried to sneak up through the underbrush as she had seen Jinx do when he was stalking a bird. She wasn't very good at it. She made an awful lot of noise, and she must have looked very funny. But it didn't matter, for there wasn't anyone to hear her; and pretty soon she was in among the corn and munching the ears with her big teeth.

When she had eaten a peck or two, she thought she'd explore a little. " Funny," she said — she had a great habit of talking to herself when she was alone — " funny there's no one around. The house looks lived in. There's a wash-tub outside, and that ax can't have been there long — it isn't rusty. Folks must be away." She walked round the house at some distance, then she walked round it a little closer, then she walked up to the kitchen window and looked in — and got the surprise of her life. For there was a little girl with a very dirty face sitting in the middle of the floor and crying. Her dress was ragged, and her tears had washed little white streaks through the grime on her cheeks, making her face look even dirtier than it was, which was almost impossible. But what surprised and horrified Mrs. Wiggins was to see that there was a long rope in the kitchen, and one end of it was around the little girl's waist, and the other was tied to a pipe under the kitchen sink.

"Good gracious sakes alive!" Mrs. Wiggins exclaimed (very strong language for a cow). "Who on *earth* has tied that poor child up like that? Perhaps an ogre has captured her and is fattening her up to eat." For Mrs. Wiggins, though only a cow, knew about ogres. There were stories about them in Grimm's *Fairy-tales,* which was one of the nicest books in Freddy's library, and Freddy had often read them aloud to the animals during the long winter evenings in the warm cow-barn.

But it couldn't be that. The little girl was too thin. Anyway, the first thing to do was to rescue her. And so Mrs. Wiggins tapped gently on the glass with the tip of her left horn.

The little girl sobbed twice, gulped, sniffed,

and looked up. Mrs. Wiggins was not handsome, and the window was so dirty and had
so many cracks in it that from the inside of
the room she looked like a funny picture of a
cow that somebody had partly erased with a
very smeary eraser; but her eyes were so big
and brown and kind and sympathetic that the
little girl wasn't afraid at all, and she jumped
up and ran as close to the window as the rope
would let her, which was about two feet, and
said: " Hello, cow! What's your name? Have
you come to take us away? "

Mrs. Wiggins nodded her head and then,
without waiting to hear what the little girl was
saying, went round to the kitchen door and
put her head against it and gave it a big push,
and the door fell in with a bang and Mrs.
Wiggins walked over it into the kitchen. But
when she got in, she found that she couldn't
do anything. She took the rope in her teeth
and pulled, but it wouldn't break, and she
tried to break the pipe that it was tied to with
her horns, but she couldn't get at it properly.

and all the while the little girl was jumping up and down in her excitement, laughing and crying, and saying: " Oh, hurry, hurry! They'll be back pretty soon, and they won't let you take us away. Please hurry! "

" Well," said Mrs. Wiggins to herself, " we're not getting anywhere this way. Not anywhere at *all!* " She thought a minute; then she went to the door and gave three long moos. This was the signal the animals had agreed on as a call for help. And, sure enough, in less than three minutes Jack and Bill and Uncle William and Charles and Henrietta came tearing across the clearing. The mice were on Bill's back, and Cecil was coming along behind as fast as he could. And Ferdinand was flying in circles overhead and acting as scout.

They all crowded into the kitchen, and while the other animals sat round and made sympathetic noises at the little girl, who was a little overpowered by seeing so many of them all at once, the mice got to work on the rope and in a few minutes had gnawed it apart. Then the little girl threw her arms around Mrs. Wiggins's neck and kissed her, which affected the cow so much that she cried. And then they went outside, where Ferdinand was on guard.

" There's a man and a woman coming across the lake in a boat," said the crow. " The man's got a gun. We've got to get out of here *quick!* "

" We're not going without that child," said Mrs. Wiggins stoutly. " She can't stay here, to be mistreated by those scoundrels. Tying her up like that! And you ought to see the bruises on her arms where they've struck her."

" Well, go get her, then," said Ferdinand irritably — for the little girl had stayed in the house — " Though what you want with her on a rescue party I don't know. She'll just be a hindrance."

" We've just rescued *her*," said Uncle William. " We can't leave her to be beaten and tied up and mistreated any more. I agree with Mrs. Wiggins."

" Well, we can't rescue everybody in the

north woods," said the crow, " or we'll never find our friends. But have it your own way. Only hurry."

So Mrs. Wiggins went into the house again. The little girl was not in the kitchen, but there were voices upstairs, and, listening, she heard a boy's voice say: " That's all foolishness. A cow couldn't come in the house and — " " But she did," the little girl interrupted. " She brought some mice and they chewed the rope apart, and they're coming to get you loose too, and then we'll go into the woods with them and live on berries and nuts and never be tied up any more."

" Good gracious me! " said Mrs. Wiggins to herself. " There's another of them! What ever will Ferdinand say to that! Well, it can't be helped. He's only a crow, anyway." And she went through into the front hall and started up the stairs.

The stairs were very narrow, so that she almost got stuck where they turned going up, and they creaked and cracked ominously, but she climbed on and presently found herself in a room with a big bay window, and in it were the little girl and a boy a few years older, who was tied up with a long rope to the foot of the bed.

Mrs. Wiggins didn't waste time. She grabbed the rope with her teeth and pulled, and the bed — which was a very handsome old colonial piece, but rather rickety — fell apart with a clatter. The little girl wanted to hug her again, but all the animals downstairs were shouting: "Hurry! Hurry!" so she pushed them through the door and, as they hurried downstairs, started to follow them. Half-way down she stuck. She pushed and heaved and panted and grunted, but only succeeded in wedging herself more firmly between wall and banisters. All the other animals had left and run off into the woods with the children to hide from the man and woman, who had pulled their boat up on the beach and were coming towards the house. Only Ferdinand had remained behind, and he was hopping about at the foot of the stairs, almost wild with exasperation, and cawing angrily at her: " Shove, can't you? Oh, I might have known it! I might have known better than to bring a cow on this expedition! Darn you, why don't you shove? "

" I *am* shoving! " panted Mrs. Wiggins. " But it's no use. Hurry, Ferdinand, or you'll be caught too. I hear them coming up the path."

With a caw of disgust Ferdinand hopped towards the door. He was only just in time, for as he spread his wings to take flight from the door-step, the woman was just coming up on the porch with the man close behind her. She jumped as the crow swished by her face, and the man exclaimed: " Well, the nerve of that crow! " and threw his gun up to his shoulder and pulled the trigger. Bang! But he had been too startled to aim carefully and he missed.

Inside the house Mrs. Wiggins was very much afraid. And when she was afraid, she was afraid all over. She shook and trembled so that the banisters rattled.

" What's that noise? " said the woman.

" I expect it's Everett," the man replied. " Tryin' to get loose from the bed."

A vindictive look came over the woman's face, and she seized a broom that stood by the door. " I'll learn him! " she shouted. " I'll learn him to — "

" ' Teach,' sister," interrupted the man. " You ' learn ' to do things, but you ' teach ' other people to — Ouch! " he broke off, for she had struck him angrily over the head with the broomstick.

" Teach or learn," she yelled, " I'll fix him! I'll tan that white skin of his'n! "

" ' His,' sister," corrected the man as he rubbed his head, but she had dashed into the house.

She was so blind with rage as she ran up the stairs that she didn't see Mrs. Wiggins until she bumped into her. Then she backed down a couple of steps and stared until it seemed to the cow as if her eyes would jump right out of her head and roll downstairs like marbles if she opened them any wider. And then with a yell of rage and fear — for of course it was rather surprising to find a cow on her front stairs — she swung up the broomstick and began beating Mrs. Wiggins over the head with it.

In her effort to escape the flying broom Mrs. Wiggins did just what she should have done before — she backed up — and at once found that she wasn't stuck any longer. She backed clumsily up the stairs with her eyes shut and her horns lowered to protect herself as well as she could, and backed into the room where the little boy had been tied, and managed to get the door shut before the woman could get in. Then she sat down against the door, so it couldn't be pushed open, and heaved a deep sigh. " Safe for a minute anyway," she said to herself. " My, what an awful woman! "

The woman pushed against the door for a while; then she ran downstairs and got her brother and they both pushed. But even the strongest brother and sister can't push open a door if a cow wants to keep it shut. So pretty soon they went back downstairs and evidently discovered that the children had escaped, for from the big bay window — which was really the nicest thing about their house and had an excellent view of the lake — the cow could see them walking about the clearing calling: " Ella! Everett! Where are you, children dear? " and promising all sorts of good things for supper if they'd only come back. " But of course," said Mrs. Wiggins to herself, " Ella and Everett know perfectly well what they'll get for supper if they really do come back. Broomstick pudding — that's what they'll get. Well, well! And how ever am I to get out of *this* mess, I'd like to know."

CHAPTER VI

THREE JOIN THE PARTY

THE man and woman — as the animals found out later — were brother and sister, and in this little house in the clearing they had been born, and in it they had lived ever since. They had very little money. They ate what they raised in the scraggly garden, and sometimes the man made a little money by acting as guide to a party of hunters from the city. The man's name was Pete, and the woman's name was Kate. Kate had never gone to school, but Pete's father had sent him to school for a year in the nearest village, and that was why Pete was always correcting Kate's grammar. He was very fond of grammar, and he had a book with all the grammatical rules in it that he had kept from his schooldays, and every night after supper he would sit down at the table with a pencil and a piece of wrapping paper and would parse sentences he found in an old newspaper. He probably knew more about syntax than anybody else in the United States.

He was always correcting Kate's grammar, which was really pretty bad, but Kate didn't like it. She thought he was showing off and being superior — which he was — and it made her mad. She would have beaten him with the broomstick when she was mad, for she was stronger than he was, but after she had beaten him, his bones ached so that he had to go to bed and couldn't work in the garden, and she had to wait on him and do the weeding and hoeing herself. So, as she had to beat somebody when she got mad, she beat the children.

The children were not their children. Their mother was Kate's sister. When she died, Kate took the children. She wanted them because she thought she could make them work for her. Pete wanted them too. They were somebody for him to teach grammar to. So the children, small as they were, had to work and learn grammar all day long. When they were good, they were spanked; and when they were bad, they were beaten. They had tried to run away several times, and that was why Kate had tied them up. She always tied them up when both she and Pete were away from the house at the same time. If the animals hadn't come along, they would probably still be living in the little house in the clearing, working and learning grammar and being spanked when they were good, and beaten when they were bad.

Of course the animals didn't learn all this until much later. But they had seen that the children were unhappy and ill-treated, and they were agreed that they must be helped to escape. Meanwhile Mrs. Wiggins must be rescued.

They had taken the children back into a dense thicket of spruce some distance from the clearing. Kate and Pete were still calling in honey-sweet tones: " Come, Everett! Come, Ella, darling! Supper's on the table, dear little ones! " While they held their council of war, the children — who of course didn't know what was being said — sat contentedly on Uncle William's back and giggled at the mice, who were trying to amuse them by dancing on their hind legs between Uncle William's ears. Ferdinand had reported that Mrs. Wiggins was back in the upstairs room with the big window and it wasn't long before they had thought up a plan for setting her free. Bill galloped off to the other side of the lake. When he got there, he came out on the shore and danced round on his hind legs until Pete caught sight of him. Bill was about the same size as Everett, and as Pete couldn't see him very clearly from that distance, he thought he was the little boy. So he jumped into the boat and started rowing across after him. Kate wanted to go too, but Pete said: " You stay and look after the cow. She's worth more to us than the children."

" But she can't get away," shouted Kate. " And those children have got a good lickin' comin' to them. Wait till I lay my hands on that there Everett! "

" How often must I tell you," said Pete wearily, pausing in his rowing, " not to say ' that there ' ? "

He was too far away to be hit with the broomstick Kate still had in her hand, so she picked up a stone and threw it at him, as he began pulling on the oars again. But she was a bad shot, — so bad a shot indeed, that the stone flew backward over her shoulder and crashed through the big bay window in the upper room and hit Mrs. Wiggins on the left horn.

The cow jumped and let out a bellow of surprise at this unexpected attack; then she looked up and saw Ferdinand perched on the window-sill. At first she thought he had thrown the stone and she started to give him a piece of her mind, and it took some time for him to persuade her that he hadn't done it. Then he said: " We're going to rescue you. But first you have to knock all the glass out of that window with your horns."

" What's that for? " exclaimed Mrs. Wiggins. " I can't jump out of this — "

" Don't ask questions," snapped the crow angrily. " Do as you're told."

So Mrs. Wiggins did as she was told as hard as she could, and pretty soon all the glass was out of the window.

Meanwhile Kate had heard the crash of smashing window-panes and came rushing up towards the house, broomstick in hand. But while she had been arguing with Pete down on the beach, Uncle William and Jack and Cecil had sneaked into the house through the kitchen door, and they were busy pulling the feather beds and pillows and mattresses off the upstairs bedsteads and throwing them out the big window, so there would be a soft pile of things for Mrs. Wiggins to jump out on. They had worked so fast that by the time Kate reached the head of the stairs, everything was all ready, and Uncle William could hold the door so she couldn't get in.

But Mrs. Wiggins didn't want to jump. She got her forefeet on the sill and looked down and shuddered. " Oh my! " she groaned. " I can't do it! It makes me dizzy just to look." And she put one hoof in front of her eyes.

Kate was banging steadily on the door with her broom-handle, and Ferdinand let out a caw of disgust. But Uncle William shook his head. " No use arguing," he said in a low voice. " All ready, Cecil? "

The porcupine nodded.

Uncle William went over and stood beside

the cow. " 'Tisn't much of a jump, really," he said. " Lean 'way out and look down. Like this, see? Why, you could almost climb down! See that window-ledge under us? " And as Mrs. Wiggins leaned out farther, he said: " All right, Cecil," and the porcupine jumped on the cow's back. With a roar of pain and surprise, Mrs. Wiggins leaped through the window and landed on her back on the pile of mattresses, with all four legs in the air.

You never can tell how anything is going to strike a cow. All the animals thought she'd be very mad. But when she had scrambled to her feet and shaken herself and found that she was safe and sound and not really hurt at all, she laughed and laughed and laughed. And when Cecil and Uncle William and Jack jumped out after her, she laughed so loud that you could hear her for six miles. She made so much noise that she frightened even Kate, who stopped banging on the door, although all she had to do now was turn the knob and walk in.

But Kate didn't stay frightened very long. She hurried downstairs and got outside just as the animals were making off towards the woods, with the feather beds piled on Mrs. Wiggins's back. Ferdinand had insisted on taking them. They'd need them, he said, in the Far North.

" Ha! " snorted Mrs. Wiggins as, at a warning caw from the crow, she looked round to see Kate running towards her, broomstick swinging threateningly. " I've had about enough of this! " And she turned round to face the enemy, lowered her horns, and pawed the ground angrily. The feather beds fell off her back, and the other animals scuttled out of the way. And then as Kate came closer, she charged.

The next thing Kate knew she was hanging in the fork of a tree about twelve feet above the ground, and the animals were disappearing into the thick woods. She shouted and called for Pete to come and help her down, but Pete was still hunting for the children on the other side of the lake. There was nothing for her to do but wait until he came back. So she made herself as comfortable as she could and tried to pass the time by inventing new punishments for the children. She had just thought up a new and more painful method of spanking and was just beginning to enjoy herself when a big black dog galloped up, stopped under her tree, and began to bark.

The dog was Jack, whom the animals had sent back as rear-guard to cover their retreat with the children. But Kate didn't know this, and as she hadn't noticed Jack particularly when the animals had run away from the house, she thought he was just a stray dog. At first his barking and jumping and tail-wagging annoyed her. Kate was one of those unfortunate persons who almost never feel anything but annoyance. When things happened, things that would please or excite or interest you or me, Kate was just annoyed. So she was annoyed now at Jack and shook her fist at him and called him names. But it's not much fun to call names or shake fists at people who don't pay any attention to it, and Jack didn't pay any attention, but sat down under the tree and looked up and smiled pleasantly and wagged his tail. So Kate stopped. And pretty soon she said: " Oh dear, I wish Pete would hurry up."

At that Jack jumped up and ran down to the beach and barked and barked, and pretty soon Pete heard him, and as he hadn't been able to find any trace of the children, he got into the boat and rowed back to see what was going on. Jack led him to the tree, and Pete got a ladder and helped Kate down.

As soon as her feet touched the ground, she got down on her knees beside Jack and hugged him and petted him. " Nice doggy," she said. " Good doggy. Ain't he a nice doggy, Pete? Why, he understands everything I say! And ain't he handsome? I never seen a handsomer dog."

Kate had never in her life said anything nice to anybody before, much less petted anybody, and Pete was so amazed that his jaw fell open and he put his hands to his head and grabbed two large handfuls of hair and pulled them right out, which was his way of expressing amazement. He even forgot to correct her grammar. But Kate took Jack back to the house and gave him a leg of venison and two roast partridges and a big dish of potatoes and gravy. In fact, she gave him everything there was in the ice-box, so that all Pete got for supper that night was four ginger-snaps and a bowl of corn flakes with a little sugar on them.

But after supper she said: " Pete, we got to get them children back."

Pete had his grammar open and was reading the " Rules Governing the Use of the Subjunctive." He held the book in one hand while the fingers of the other felt round the inside of the bowl to pick out the last crumbs of corn flakes. " Those," he said absently, and went on reading.

Kate pulled the book away from him.

" Listen to me," she said. " We got to follow them children. Tomorrow'll be too late."

" We can't follow them tonight," said Pete. " We can't see the trail."

" We don't need to see it," she replied. " What's this dog for, I'd like to know? Let him smell one of Everett's shoes; he'll follow 'em all right."

" H'm, that's an idea," said Pete. " They can't have got far. And maybe we can find the cow, too."

" We've got to find all of 'em," said Kate. " With the children to do the work, and the cow to give milk and cream and butter, we'll be settin' pretty. But we'll set mighty uncomfortable if we don't find 'em."

" Sit," said Pete. But the idea of having a little milk on his corn flakes occasionally was pleasant, so he got up and lit a lantern while Kate went after one of Everett's shoes.

As soon as Jack had smelt the shoe, he started off, nose to ground, like a bloodhound. Kate and Pete were delighted. They wouldn't have been so happy if they had known that they were being led in exactly the opposite direction from the one the children had taken. Jack had intended to make the chase as difficult as possible for them — to lead them through swamps and briers and up steep hills; but he was kind-hearted, like most dogs, and after they had fed him and treated him so well, he couldn't bear to be meaner than he had to. So after they had followed him steadily for two hours, he decided to put an end to the game and get back to his friends.

They were going along the side of a hill when he noticed by the light of Pete's lantern a heap of big boulders and under them a hole that might have been the mouth of a cave. He gave a sharp yelp, as if the scent was getting very hot, and dashed off towards the opening; then he stopped a yard or two short of it, barking short eager barks, as if he knew the children were inside.

But to his surprise and disappointment neither Pete nor Kate showed any desire to go into the cave. He had hoped that they would, and then he could run away and re-join his friends. There was a queer smell about the cave, too, now that he was close to it — a strong smell that he had never smelt before. He went a little nearer to investigate, and then gave a sharp yelp of surprise, for out of the hole came lumbering a huge black shape with long white teeth in a snarling mouth and eyes that glowed red in the lantern-light.

Right there Jack decided that he had done enough for one evening, and he turned round and started home. His first jump took him three yards past his companions, who were both trying to climb the same tree, and his second jump took him over the branches of a fallen hemlock, and his third jump scared into fits an old grandfather rabbit who had come out to forage for a late supper, and who reached home trembling and shaking an hour later and took to his bed for three weeks. By his fourth jump Jack had got into his stride, and he raced on over fallen trees and through

106

bushes and briers and along deer paths, as fast as he could go, for by the thumping and swishing and crackling behind him he knew that that terrible animal was close on his heels.

Pretty soon he heard a hoarse voice behind him: " Hey, wait a minute."

" Yes, I will! " the dog jeered over his shoulder, without slackening his pace.

" Wait a minute," repeated the other animal. " I want to talk to you."

" Well, go on," barked Jack. " I'm listening."

" Don't be funny," replied the other crossly. " How can I talk this way? "

" You seem to be doing pretty well," said Jack.

" Oh, you make me tired! " returned the pursuer.

" Just what I'm trying to do," snapped Jack. Then he laughed. " That was a pretty good one, eh what? " he inquired.

" Oh, you're a wit all right," grunted the other. " But what's the sense of all this

Pretty soon he heard a hoarse voice behind him, "*Hey, wait a minute*"

running? I'm not chasing you. I'm running away too."

" Running away from an empty cupboard," said Jack. " I know. You aren't chasing me. You're taking your supper out for a little exercise."

" Nonsense," grumbled the pursuer. " Bears don't eat dogs."

" Hey! " barked Jack in surprise. " Are you a bear? " But still he didn't slow up.

" Sure I am," came the reply. " But I can't talk like this. Stop and sit down a minute."

" You stop first," said Jack, leaping over a little stream.

" Yes, and you'll go on running," objected the bear as he splashed through the shallow water.

" No, I won't. I'll take two more jumps after you stop, and then I'll stop. And then we can talk if you want to so bad."

So they worked it that way.

" Now," said the bear, when they had got

their breath back and were sitting facing each other some distance apart in the dark woods, " what I wanted to say to you was this: I don't suppose you're any friend to that man and woman you came to my cave with or you'd have stayed with them when I came out. Is that so? "

" They're no friends of mine," said Jack.

" Good. They're no friends of mine either. They've been hunting me with a gun ever since I came into these parts, three years ago. It's got so I can hardly stick my nose outside my cave nowadays without hearing that gun go bang and feeling a bullet whiz through my fur. Up to now I've been safe in the cave, but now they know where it is, I shan't be able to live there any longer. And being as you're the one that brought 'em there — "

" Gosh, I'm sorry," said Jack. " I didn't know — "

" I know you didn't," said the bear. " But you brought 'em, anyway. I don't bear any grudge, but it seems to me you have a certain responsibility, and for that reason maybe you'd be willing to help me."

"Sure," said Jack heartily, " anything I can do."

" Well, then," said the bear, " I'm a peaceable animal. What I want is a nice quiet home and three square meals a day — nothing fancy, you understand, just a comfortable den and good plain food. But the woods are no place for bears nowadays — haven't been since my grandfather was a cub. There's too much talk in the cities nowadays about back to nature. I don't object to men going back to nature, but I don't see why they have to take a gun with them. This time of year there are more hunters in the woods than there are animals. What I want is peace and quiet. And I thought maybe you could help me find it."

" Why, so I can," said Jack — " or could if I weren't going in the opposite direction. There's just the place on the farm where I live — a big wood lot that nobody ever goes into, and I'm sure Mr. Bean would let you live there. Only you see . . ." And he explained about the rescue party.

The bear was greatly interested. " I'd like to meet your friends," he said. " They sound like a fine lot of animals."

" Oh, they're all right," said Jack. " They're a good lot of fellows. I'd like to have you meet them if you want to come along with me."

" Sure," said the bear. " Sure, I'd like to. And maybe — well, I've been thinking that maybe I could go along with you on this trip. I'm strong, and I don't mind the cold, and my knowledge of the woods might be of use to you. At least I'd be more of a help than a hindrance. What do you think? "

" Why, it's all right with me," said Jack. " Of course Ferdinand's the leader; he'd have to decide. If you went, you could come back home with us, too."

" That's what I was thinking," said the bear. " And, to tell you the truth, if I don't go with you, I don't know what I will do."

" Well, come along then," said the dog.

"We've got some distance to go. Ha ha!" He laughed in two or three short little barks. "To think I thought you were chasing me, and all the time you were just running away too! But you certainly gave me a scare."

"I'm sorry for that," said the bear. "But I'll try to make it up to you some time."

CHAPTER VII
A LECTURE TOUR IN THE NORTH WOODS

EVEN Ferdinand was pleased at the addition of the bear to their party, and indeed he was very useful, for he knew all the edible berries and roots that the woods animals live on, and that they, as farm-bred animals, had never learned anything about. He was very nervous for a day or two, until he was sure that Kate and Pete were not pursuing them, but then he brightened up and made himself quite agreeable.

Ella and Everett were very happy. They had got so accustomed to being spanked at least three times a day that they thought it was a regular part of living, like getting up and going to bed, and at first they missed it. So for the first few days they spanked each other every morning before breakfast. But there were so many other things to do and to see that pretty soon they forgot all about it. They rode on Mrs. Wiggins's back and on Uncle William's back and on the bear's back, and they raced through the woods with Jack after imaginary rabbits and tigers and played tag with Charles and Henrietta. All the animals grew very fond of them; even Ferdinand, who liked himself so well that he couldn't like anybody else very much, occasionally flew down and perched on their shoulders, although he said he only did it to get his feet warm.

Poor Cecil was the only one who couldn't play with them. He wanted to awfully, but he was too prickly. It made him very sad, and he used to cry sometimes at night thinking about it. But he was a sensible porcupine and very soon decided that it was silly to cry about something he couldn't help; and then, as usually happens, he found that he could have a perfectly good time with them even though he did have to be careful not to let them touch him.

As they went on north, the winter came down to meet them. It grew colder and colder. Finally one morning Charles stuck his head out from under the feather bed where he had been sleeping all snug and warm, in order to crow and wake the others up. He kept his eyes shut, for he was very sleepy, but when he opened his beak to crow, no sound came out and his mouth was full of something soft and cold. That woke him wide awake at once, and his eyes flew open. And then he really was scared for a minute, for there was only a grey-ish whiteness everywhere; he could see nothing, not even the feather bed.

With a muffled squawk he wriggled out and jumped and flapped his wings agitatedly, and the whiteness broke up into flakes and dust and whirled about his head, and when it at last settled, he saw what had really happened: he had been sleeping under a blanket of snow, six inches thick, that had fallen during the night.

Charles grinned sheepishly and shivered and hopped up on to a low branch. Of course! They had been snowed under. Those two big white mounds with smaller mounds between them were Uncle William and the bear, who slept one on each side of the children to keep them warm. That other big mound was Mrs. Wiggins; he could hear her snoring gently and see a little whirl of snow fly up with every breath from where her nose was; and one horn was sticking out. And beyond were lower mounds where the other animals were snoozing away in their feather beds. Yes, and up on that spruce limb was Ferdinand, his head under his wing, and a little heap of snow piled up between his shoulders. Charles threw back his head and flapped his wings and gave a loud, shrill crow.

At once the snow blanket began to heave and bulge and heads and legs and horns stuck out through it, and presently all the animals were on their feet, shaking snow out of their fur, their noses steaming like so many tea-kettles in the cold morning air.

" My gracious! " said Mrs. Wiggins. " This is winter with a vengeance! "

Ferdinand cawed derisively. " Winter! " he exclaimed. " Why this is nothing — *nothing* to what's coming. Maybe you animals'll wake up to the fact some time that this isn't any picnic we're going on."

" Oh my goodness! " said the cow. " Who said it was? Can't I make a single remark about the weather without your jumping all over me? "

" Oh, who's jumping all over you? " snapped the crow. " I just get sick of hearing you complain when there isn't anything to complain about."

" I'm complaining about you," retorted Mrs. Wiggins, " and I guess anyone here will

118

bear me out that there's something to complain about."

" He, he! " snickered the goat. " Laugh that one off, Ferd. That's a hot one, that is."

Bill's laughter made the crow mad. He hopped down to the ground. " Look here," he said, " if there's any dissatisfaction with me as leader of this expedition, I want to know about it now."

" No, no! " said all the animals. " We're perfectly satisfied. You're a fine leader. Mrs. Wiggins didn't mean anything." But Ferdinand walked straight up to the cow. " And how about you? " he asked, looking her straight in the eye.

" My goodness! " she said again. " This has all come up very suddenly. I didn't really mean anything against you, Ferdinand."

" Then you've no complaint to make? " he demanded.

Now, Mrs. Wiggins was very good-natured, and she didn't want to hurt anybody's feelings, but she didn't see why she should have to back down when she hadn't really done anything. So she said boldly: " Yes, I have."

" All right," said Ferdinand grimly. " Out with it."

The cow hesitated. She couldn't really think of anything she had against the crow, except that he was bad-tempered and bossy and disagreeable, and she didn't want to use any of those words because she was afraid they might make him feel bad. If she could only think of one that didn't mean quite so much; even one that didn't mean anything at all would be better. . . . And then she suddenly remembered a word that she had heard in a story that Freddy had been reading out loud one night in the cow-barn. She didn't know what it meant, but it sounded like the right kind of word. So she said: " Well, if you want to know, I think you're too sophisticated."

At this unexpected word Ferdinand gave a little jump. Then he opened his beak to say something, but as he didn't know what the word meant, he couldn't think of any way to argue against it, and he just stood there with his beak open, looking very foolish.

Mrs. Wiggins turned to the other animals. " Isn't he too sophisticated? " she asked, and as none of them wanted to admit that he didn't know what the word meant, they all nodded and said yes.

Poor Ferdinand managed to pull his wits together somewhat. " I am *not* sophisticated! " he exclaimed. " I've been perfectly open and above-board about everything, and — "

" Oh, that isn't what I mean at all," said the cow; and as she didn't know what she did mean, it was perfectly true.

" Well, what do you mean, then? " asked the harassed crow.

" Just what I say," returned Mrs. Wiggins. She appealed to the others. " Isn't it perfectly plain? " And they all nodded emphatically and said: " Yes, yes. Perfectly."

" Well, it isn't what *I* mean by sophisticated," said Ferdinand, now thoroughly mixed up.

" Just what *do* you mean by it? " asked the cow coldly.

And at that the crow just turned round and walked off with his shoulders hunched up and didn't come near the others for the rest of the day. But it had done him some good, as Mrs. Wiggins observed with satisfaction, for from that time on he treated her with marked respect.

They went on through the snowy woods for several days, and the snow came down in thick flakes and got deeper and deeper and harder and harder to walk through. The big animals didn't mind it much, but the smaller animals and Charles and Henrietta and the children had to ride most of the time; and the children in particular were cold because they didn't have warm enough clothing. They were only warm at night when they snuggled down under a feather bed between Uncle William and the bear. Moreover, it was a good deal harder to find enough food, now that the country was all covered with snow.

So pretty soon the animals began to grumble. If Ferdinand was such a good leader, they said, he ought to be able to keep them from starving or freezing. They wouldn't be much good to the animals they had come to rescue if they starved or froze stiff. And if the snow got much deeper, how were they going to travel at all? They asked Ferdinand these questions. "You've been here before," they said. "How did you get food?"

"We took it with us in the old phaeton," said the crow.

"How did you keep warm?"

"We took blankets with us and wrapped them around us."

"And how did you walk over the deep snow?"

"We made snowshoes," said the crow. "I can show you how to do that."

"H'm," said Jack thoughtfully. "That takes care of one thing. But what are we going to do for food and clothing?"

" Yes," said Henrietta. " Why didn't you tell us all this in the first place, when we started out? You didn't think about anybody but yourself. You don't mind the cold the way we do, and you can fly through the air and live on nuts and things that you steal from squirrels and chipmunks. It's very easy for *you*. But why didn't you think about *us?* A fine leader you are! "

Ferdinand looked round out of the corners of his eyes at his comrades. It was perfectly true. When he had come back to organize the rescue party, he had been so full of his own importance that he had forgotten all about such little matters as proper food and clothing. He'd have to think of something pretty quickly, or they'd reduce him to the ranks and elect a new leader. He could see them looking meaningly at one another — even his bosom friend, Bill, was shaking his head very seriously and avoided his eye — and he could hear a *buzz-buzz* as they whispered to each other: " Too sophisticated. Yes, yes; too sophisticated." Then suddenly an idea came to him. He ruffled out his feathers.

" My friends," he said importantly, " on the face of it, what you allege against me seems to be true. I did *not* see fit to burden us with large stores of food and clothing, which would seriously have hampered us. There is a better way to get what we need. There are reasons why I did not tell you about it before — "

Bill giggled audibly. " I'll say there were! " he muttered coarsely; but Ferdinand gave him a hard look and he subsided, though his beard continued to tremble with subdued laughter.

" The time, however," continued the crow, " has now come. As you have seen, these woods are full of birds and animals — creatures of little experience, who have never known much about anything but their small woodland affairs and are intensely curious about the outside world. What's the one thing we can give them that they haven't got? Why, our experience of the outside world, of course. We've travelled; we've been everywhere and done everything; we know life. We can sell that knowledge for the things we need."

At this point Bill snickered again. " You mean you're going to trade your good advice for food? " he asked. " Well, if these animals are anything like me, you won't get many customers. My experience is that you can get all the good advice you want from your relatives. You don't have to go outside the family. And you don't have to pay for it, either. Sell advice indeed! Huh! Might as well try to sell Cecil here a quill toothpick! "

" That was *not* what I meant," said Ferdinand coldly, " and now that this unseemly interruption is over, I will tell you that my idea was simply this: to give a series of lectures of various kinds, admission to which will be paid in articles of food or clothing."

" That's a good idea all right," said Uncle William, " as far as food goes. But how do you expect to get blankets and clothing for the children? These woods animals haven't got such things."

" They'll find them," said the crow confidently. " Why, suppose you wanted to find an old coat for this boy to wear. I mean if you were at home, in your own stable. Couldn't you do it? "

" Why, yes, as a matter of fact, I could," replied the horse. " There's a couple of old overcoats down in the tool-shed. But that's different. Up here in the woods — "

" Up here in the woods it's just the same," said Ferdinand. " There are hunters and campers and trappers and lumbermen, and they're always throwing away things."

" But how can you find them, in all these square miles of trees? "

" *You* couldn't. That's just the point. But take one of these deer. He knows every square inch of ground for miles. If there's an old coat within five miles of here, he'll know it. If there isn't, he'll have a friend over the hill who'll know where there is one. And so on."

" Why not have a lecture tonight? " said Charles. " I have one, you know, that I

127

prepared after our trip to Florida. 'A Trip to the Sunny Southland.' And that one about Washington: 'How Our Legislators Live.' That was very well received. And — "

" Oh, be still! " said Henrietta. " Nobody wants to hear you lecture If they'd heard you talk as much as I have, they'd pay to stay away."

" But that's the point: they haven't! " said Charles triumphantly.

" Well, they will! " said his wife sarcastically. " Believe me, if there's an animal between here and the pole that doesn't know your life-history by the time the winter's over, I'll be surprised."

Charles hung his head, but Ferdinand came to his rescue. " I think it's a good idea for Charles to deliver his Florida talk tonight," he said. " We'll stay here today and make snowshoes. I'll go notify those chickadees over in that pine there, and they'll tell all the other birds and animals. I bet we have a big attendance."

For the rest of the day under the crow's supervision the travellers gnawed down small saplings and tore off strips of bark, which they bent and tied into rough snowshoes. Charles alone was absent. He had retired into a thicket where he could rehearse his speech privately, and every now and then phrases would float out to the workers and they would smile at each other. "I have been asked. . . . A very unpretentious task, my friends. . . . Undaunted I flew at the alligator and pecked him so that he winced. 'Sir,' I said. . . . With my skill in debate, I of course won the prize without difficulty. . . ." And so on.

The lecture that evening, however, was a great success. A large and enthusiastic audience of deer, coons, foxes, rabbits, porcupines, and skunks hung breathlessly on Charles's words, rocked with laughter at his sallies, and cheered wildly at the stories of hairbreadth escapes — which, as he said afterwards, while not strictly true, were founded on fact. The other members of the rescue party, with the exception of the children, Henrietta, and the bear, acted as ushers at the beginning, but sneaked off when he began to talk and played twenty questions until the meeting broke up. They had heard it all so many times that they felt they just couldn't stand it again, and, as Ferdinand said: " We're all fond of Charles, but he *is* tiresome when he gets to talking about himself, and if we stay, we'll get so irritated we'll throw things, and that wouldn't do."

The children stayed, and at first they were so delighted to have so many animals around them that they were a little noisy, but although they didn't understand what Charles was saying, they understood pretty soon that he was making a speech, and, being considerate children, they sat quietly and applauded when the others applauded, and at the end when some of the animals went up to shake hands with the lecturer, they went up too.

The bear stayed, partly because he hadn't heard Charles talk before, and partly because two of his cousins whom he hadn't seen in a long time came to the lecture. He sat with them in the front row, but he was so glad to see them again that he talked a good deal and had to be shushed by the other animals several times before he would keep still.

As for Henrietta, although in private she scolded her husband soundly at every opportunity, she was really very proud of him and would fly at anyone else who ventured even the slightest criticism of him, and so tonight she perched quite close beside him on the low branch from which he spoke, and admired him so openly and applauded so enthusiastically that it embarrased even Charles a little.

" Not so loud! " he whispered to her once when she continued stamping and shouting " Bravo! " long after the audience had stopped. " They'll think it's funny."

" They don't know I'm your wife," she muttered.

" They'll think I hired you to applaud," he replied.

" Oh, shut up and go on with your talk," she whispered angrily. Then she shouted " Bravo! " again and looked him defiantly in the eye. And Charles went hastily on with the lecture.

The box-office, presided over by Ferdinand, took in enough food to feed them for a week, a heavy flannel shirt checquered in big red and black squares, two old sweaters, four pairs of lumbermen's heavy socks, a knitted bed jacket with pink ribbons, a whisk broom, two boxes of matches, a bottle of hair-tonic, and a postage-stamp album containing a complete collection of the stamps of the British colonies. The woods animals had found these various articles at different times and had hidden them away for no particular reason, as animals do. Everett put on the flannel shirt, which came down to his heels, and Ella wore one of the sweaters, which she had to hold up so she wouldn't trip over it, and they both put on the heavy socks, which were much too large, so that they looked very funny. But they didn't care, for they were warm.

From that day on, the trip became more of a lecture tour than a rescue expedition. The news of their coming ran ahead of them, and every ten miles or so they would be met by a committee of animals who wanted to engage them to give a series of lectures in their territory. But of course they were in a hurry, so they decided that they could give only one lecture in each place, and if the animals wanted to hear a different talk, they would have to travel along with them to the next stop. Many animals did this, and the result was that although the snow soon got very deep, they seldom had to use their snowshoes, for in order to pay their admission to the next lecture, the animals who travelled with them would go on ahead and break trail for them. When fifty to a hundred moose and deer and bear had tramped over a trail, it was almost as hard and smooth as a state road.

Of course Charles couldn't do all the lecturing. He always talked so loud that he was hoarse for a week after one lecture. " He gives himself too much," said Henrietta. So Uncle William talked on " Life under the Big Top," which was recollections of his year with a circus, and Bill had a humorous talk, " Here and There in Rural New York," which was very well received, and Jack spoke on " Our Civilization: Whither Bound? " which was rather philosophical and not so popular among the younger woods animals. After a time he gave that up and talked on " How to Live with Human Beings," a good many of the facts for which he got from the mice. Ferdinand talked on " Life in a Southern Tree-top," and Mrs. Wiggins had two topics: " The Inside of the Dairy Business " and " From Cow-barn to White House," which told of her trip to Washington, where she shook hands with the President. She had a homely humour which always went well with the crowd, and always spoke extempore, which means that she never

134

knew what she was going to say until after she had said it. Her lectures were always well attended, partly, of course, because many of the woods animals had never seen a cow before. Later, too, they got up some debates, the most popular of which was one between the bear and Uncle William called " Farm vs. Forest." Uncle William argued that life on the farm was best, and the bear took the opposite view. But to please the woods audience it was arranged beforehand that the bear should win.

And so the gallant little band went on northward, travelling swiftly on the road that the woods animals made for them. They were always on the alert for news of their friends, and at the end of each lecture the speaker would explain the purpose of the expedition and appeal to his audience for news of the whaling ship and the lost animals. But although among the birds and the deer there were many rumours of a party of strange animals who had been seen here and there in the arctic regions, there was no real news.

All these rumours seemed to come from the north, however, so they knew they were still travelling in the right direction.

CHAPTER VIII
JACK AND CHARLES GET INTO TROUBLE

AND now the winter came down upon them in earnest. The snow was like powdered ice, the trees snapped and cracked in the cold, and though at night under their feather beds they were snug and comfortable, during the day they had to keep moving briskly to keep warm. And as it got colder, it got more and more difficult to get the bear up in the morning, because he was accustomed to crawling into his hole and sleeping all winter, and no matter how loud Charles crowed, he just went on snoring comfortably, and if they pulled the covers all off him, he just curled up tighter and grunted and went on sleeping. They tried shaking him, but he was so big and heavy and they had to shake so long before he woke up that they were all tired out afterwards and had to rest for an hour before they could start the day's march. Then one morning when she was helping to shake him awake, Mrs. Wiggins happened to stick one horn into his ribs. And immediately the bear's eyes flew open and he gave a wriggle and a silly laugh and shouted: " Ugh! Stop that tickling! "

Mrs. Wiggins sat back on her haunches and bellowed with laughter. " Hey! Animals! " she gasped. " He's ticklish! Can you imagine that — a ticklish bear? " But while she was laughing, he had gone back to sleep. So she tickled him again, until he rolled round, giggling and pawing the air and begging her to stop. And this time she woke him up thoroughly. After that it was Mrs. Wiggins's job to get the bear up every morning.

The animals slept very soundly at night, and, with the feather beds over their ears, they couldn't hear anything that went on in the forest around them. But very early one morning Jack and Charles, who were sleeping next to Uncle William, woke up, feeling cold, to find that the horse had dragged the covers off them in his sleep.

Jack got one corner in his teeth and tried to drag them back, but Uncle William was lying on them.

" We'll have to wake him up," said Charles.

" We'll disturb everybody if we do," replied the dog. " You know how he snorts when he wakes up."

" Well, it can't be helped," said the rooster sharply. " It won't be time to get up for nearly two hours yet, and I don't propose to lie here and freeze just because that big lump has — "

" Listen! " said Jack.

From the dark forest came a long-drawn howl.

" Sounds like a dog," said Charles. " But

dogs always live with people, don't they? And there aren't any people for miles."

"Maybe he's lost," said Jack. "I tell you what we'll do. You aren't sleepy any more, are you?"

"Not after all this row," said Charles grumpily.

"Well then, let's take a little walk and see if we can find him. If he's lost, maybe we can put him on the road home."

Charles grumbled a little, but he was just as curious to know about the strange dog as Jack was, so presently they set out, leaving their friends snoring comfortably away in their beds. The snow was packed so hard that even the rooster could walk on it without sinking in, but as it made his feet cold, he preferred to ride on Jack's back. As soon as they were a little way from the camp, Jack gave a few barks, to let the other dog know they were coming, and was answered after a minute with some sharp yelps.

"Maybe he's caught in a trap," said

140

Charles. " Anyway, he didn't sound very far away. But what are those funny noises in the bushes? "

" I don't know," Jack replied. " I've noticed them on both sides of us. It's as if somebody were going along beside us, keeping out of sight. But of course that's impossible. It must be the snow. There's a funny smell, though. D'you notice it? "

" Yes. I've been wondering what it was," said Charles. This wasn't true, for roosters can't smell at all. Even the very finest perfume would be wasted on them. But they're so vain that they never want to admit that there's anything they can't do, and that was why Charles said yes.

" Smells like bear a little, and like dog a little," said Jack reflectively, " yet it isn't either. I wonder — Hello! Here he is! " For they had come out into an open glade, in the middle of which a very big shaggy dog was lying in the snow.

" How do you do? " said Jack politely. " We

thought we heard you howl, and we wondered if there was anything we could do for you. We thought perhaps you were lost, and although we're strangers in this part of the country ourselves, we can perhaps help to put you on the right road."

" Thank you, thank you. Very kind, I'm sure," said the other. He got up and shook the snow from his coat, which was thick and shaggy, and greyish tan in colour. He smiled as he spoke, but his eyes, which were slanting and sly, did not smile, and his teeth were long and white. Charles shifted his feet uneasily on Jack's back and whispered: " I don't like this fellow. I don't like the way he looks at me. He makes me feel as if I didn't have any feathers on."

" Yes, yes," the other continued as he came closer to them. " Very kind indeed. You're a farm dog, I expect? "

" Yes," said Jack. " We're travelling with a party of friends — bound for the north pole. My friend and I were just wondering what kind of dog you were. A very rare species, no doubt. We've never seen a dog like you before."

"Never seen — No, I dare say you haven't," said the stranger absently. "The north pole! Well, well! How interesting!" He came very close and, putting up his nose, sniffed at Charles so intently that the rooster felt the goose-flesh prickling on his back between his wings. "And your friend is a rooster? Yes, yes; I know the smell " — he licked his chops — "though it's a long time since — " He broke off. "Ah, well; we'll speak of that later. I must tell you how much I appreciate your thoughtfulness in coming out to find me. I had scarcely hoped — " He broke off again and smiled as if very much pleased with himself.

"Well," said Jack bluntly, "I see you're not in trouble, and you're evidently not lost, so I guess there isn't anything we can do for you, and we'd better be getting back to our friends. If you'd care to come back and have

143

a bite of breakfast with us, I know our friends would be pleased."

"Thanks so much," replied the other; "you're too kind. But I can't permit your generosity to go unrewarded. I really must insist on your staying and having breakfast with me and *my* friends. I'm sure they'll be ever so much more pleased to see *you* than *your* friends would be to see *me*." And he laughed outright.

"*Your* friends?" exclaimed Jack. "But I thought you — "

"Forgive me," said the stranger. "In the pleasure of meeting you I had forgotten that I was neglecting to present them to you." He raised his nose and sent forth a long, doleful howl, and immediately there was a rustling in the bushes all about them, and the two travellers found themselves the centre of a ring of huge shaggy grey dogs, all sitting on their haunches and smiling at them with very hungry-looking jaws.

Too late Jack realized that he had walked

straight into a trap, although what kind of a trap it was, and what sort of animals these were, he had no idea. He could feel Charles trembling violently, but he managed to keep his presence of mind.

"Well, well," he said, "I'm very glad to meet them, I'm sure. But I don't think I've seen any of them at any of our lectures, have I?"

The other laughed, a little less politely this time. "No," he said, "I don't think you have. And you won't see them at any lectures in the future. In fact, you're not likely to attend any future lectures yourself, unless you do exactly as we tell you to. Eh, boys?" And he looked round at his friends, who all grinned and licked their chops expectantly.

In spite of his danger, Jack began to get mad. It was beginning to get light now, and he could see that these animals were really a very ferocious-looking crew. But although it was high time his own friends were up and about the business of getting breakfast, he knew that without Charles to wake them they would probably sleep late, and it would be an hour or more before they would become alarmed at his absence and set out to look for him. He must gain as much time as he could. " I don't know what you're talking about," he said, " but I suppose it's some sort of a joke, for I don't believe for a minute that you intend to try to keep us here against our will. We've never done you any harm — " But he got no further, for the leader suddenly lifted his muzzle and barked a sharp command. Immediately the other animals got to their feet and closed in around their prisoners.

" Come," said the leader. " We've stayed here long enough. You come with us."

Jack looked round at the ring of sharp teeth and menacing eyes. " All right," he said. " But if any harm comes to us, you'll be sorry."

Two or three of the captors laughed at this as they moved off, but the leader said: " You'll come to no harm if you go quietly and do as we say. Forward, march! " And the animals wheeled like a squad of soldiers and marched their prisoners off into the forest.

As Jack walked along over the frozen snow, listening to the laughter and coarse jokes of his guards, an idea came to him. " Get up on my head, Charles," he said in a low voice.

Charles was so frightened that at first he paid no attention, but kept on shivering and muttering: " Oh dear! Oh dear me! Whatever will Henrietta do without me? And my eighteen little ones at home; shall I never see them again? Oh, what a sad and untimely end to a useful and glorious life! " But presently, after Jack had repeated his order several times, Charles obeyed. Most of the trees in this part of the forest were tall and had no branches for twenty or thirty feet up, but pretty soon they passed through a clump of spruces whose low boughs were just over their heads. " Now, Charles! Jump when I tell you," whispered Jack. Before the other animals realized what he was doing, he stopped, shouted: " Jump! " and, rearing up on his hind legs, fairly tossed the fluttering rooster up on to one of the limbs. " Now crow for all you're worth! " he cried.

And Charles crowed as he had never crowed before. His feet slipping and sliding on the ice-covered limb, his tail feathers snapped at by the mob of infuriated animals, who were leaping up beneath him and trying to pull him down, he crowed until the woods echoed for miles, and elk and bears and beaver and foxes and weasels, going about their morning business in distant parts of the forest, paused and lifted their heads and said: " Is that someone singing? What a beautiful voice! "

But it did not last for long. The limb was so slippery that Charles could not hop higher up on it and so get out of reach of his pursuers, and presently one of them caught him by the wing and pulled him roughly down. Jack had had no chance to escape, for two of the largest of the animals had stood on each side of him while the others were trying to recapture Charles, and he knew that if he tried

" Is that someone singing? "

to run, they would stop him. Now one of them picked up Charles carefully and replaced him on Jack's back, and the leader came up and spoke to him.

"Another little trick like that," he said, "and there won't be enough of you left in five minutes to make soup of. I shan't warn you again."

But the prisoners did not need the warning. They were thoroughly discouraged.

In about two hours they came to a cave, which was evidently the headquarters of their captors. Charles shuddered violently as he saw the bones lying about the outside of the cave. "Those are rooster bones, some of them," he groaned. "Oh, I feel in my own bones that I shall never see my eighteen little ones again."

There were several large rooms in the cave and they were led through a narrow doorway into one of these, and a guard was posted outside. After a while the leader of the animals came in. "Now," he said, "we can have a little talk, and I'll tell you what I want you to do.

If **you** agree to do it, we'll let you go. If you don't, we'll eat you. You can take your choice."

" We don't want to be eaten," said Jack.

" All right, then. Now listen to me. We've been following you for several days. There are a little boy and a little girl in your party. We want them. If you will promise to bring them to us, we'll let you go right away. If you won't promise — " He smiled politely, but unpleasantly. " Well, in that case, my dear dog, I'm afraid that you and your young feathered friend here — "

" Oh, please! " interrupted Charles. " Don't say it again."

" Very well. But make up your minds quickly. My friends are impatient — and hungry."

" But," said Jack, " suppose we promise and then just go away and don't bring them to you."

" Oh, you won't do that," said the other. " I fancy that I am a better judge of animal

151

nature than to think that of you. Your friend might do it, but no dog would. No dog will tell a lie, even to save his own skin."

This was perfectly true. No dog in the history of the world has ever been known to tell a lie, and that is why man has selected the dog as his chief friend among the animals.

"What do you want the children for?" asked Jack. "Are you going to eat *them?*"

"Oh, my dear fellow!" exclaimed the other. "How could you dream of such a thing? Certainly not! W — ah — well, it's a little difficult to explain. You see — "

"We see perfectly well," interrupted Jack. "And we're not going to do it. You can eat us if you want to. But wait till our friends find out about it. Eh, Charles?"

"You bet!" said Charles. Like all roosters, he had plenty of courage when he was angry, and the suggestion that they should betray their friends had made him good and mad. "You great big bully, you! You cheap, sneaky baby-eater! When they get through with you, there won't be enough left to stop up a key-hole with. You get out of here! " And he flew at the astonished animal, clawing and pecking at his eyes, and drove him out of the room into the other part of the cave.

"There, Jack," he said as he smoothed down his ruffled feathers, " I guess I fixed him! Now all we've got to do is stand at the doorway. It's narrow and only one of them can get at us at a time. Let's see 'em try to eat us up! "

But Jack was gloomy. " That's all right for a while," he said, " but by and by we'll have to get some sleep, and then they can sneak in and overpower us."

" Well, anyway," said the rooster, " we can hold them off for a while, and maybe Uncle William and Mrs. Wiggins and the rest of them will get here by then."

" Maybe," said Jack hopelessly. " Well, it's all we can do."

At that moment the sharp muzzle of their enemy appeared again in the doorway. " Keep back! " Charles warned him. But he did not try to come in.

" Oh sure, I'll keep back," he snarled, glaring at them with his wicked yellow eyes. " We can wait. We'll have a better appetite tomorrow than we've got today. Huh! We wouldn't let you go now anyway. No rooster can play tricks on a wolf and get away with it." And he disappeared.

" Wolf! " exclaimed Jack. " Whew! We *are* in a mess if these are wolves. I've never seen one before, but I've heard about them. They're the worst animals in the woods. They hunt in packs, and they'll attack and eat any animal that isn't strong enough to defend himself. They even eat people sometimes."

" Eat people! " exclaimed Charles. " I never heard of such a thing! Why, I can't believe it, Jack; it just isn't done! Haven't they any sense of decency? "

" What do you suppose they want the children for? " asked Jack.

" Well, perhaps you're right," replied the

rooster. " The only wolf I ever heard of was the one in the story Freddy read us once, the one that pretended he was the little girl's grandmother and ate her up. But I thought that was just a fairy-story."

" Red Riding-hood," said Jack. " Well, they'll eat *us* up all right, and don't you forget it."

" I'd like to forget it, for a while anyway," said Charles. " Are you sleepy? "

" Beginning to be," said Jack. " It's so quiet here, and I didn't have my sleep out this morning. Suppose you tell a story to while away the time and keep us awake. They'll surely come to rescue us before long."

" All right," replied the rooster. " Keep your eye on the door.

" Once upon a time there was a very handsome dog named John, and he lived . . ."

CHAPTER IX
A FIGHT IN THE FOREST

WHEN Charles had crowed so loud and long and despairingly for help, the animals had all been asleep, and Mrs. Wiggins was snoring so loudly that none of them heard him. None, that is, except Henrietta. But Charles was Henrietta's husband, and somehow that familiar voice, raised in fear and entreaty, had penetrated her dreams. She woke and poked her head out from under the feather bed just in time to hear the last " Help! " he uttered before the wolves pulled him down. In an instant she was out of bed, clucking excitedly, and pecking sharply at Mrs. Wiggins's nose.

"Wake up!" she cried. "Charles is in trouble! Something awful is going on; I know it! Oh, wake up, animals! Wake up and help me!"

"Wha's 'at?" murmured Mrs. Wiggins sleepily. "Trouble? Wha's a trouble? Fly on my nose, tha's a trouble. Go 'way, fly." And she shook her head, sighed, and went to sleep again.

But Henrietta kept right on squawking and pecking, and before long all the animals were on their feet and listening to her story.

"No time to waste," said Uncle William. "I've warned Charles not to wander away from the camp. He could easily get lost, and there are wildcats in these woods, who'd like nothing better than a fat rooster for breakfast."

"Don't you call my husband fat!" exclaimed the hen. "Poking fun at him when he's in trouble, and — "

"I beg your pardon," said the horse. "I mis-spoke myself. Charles has a very handsome and elegant figure; I've often commented upon it. But look, here are his tracks, and here are Jack's with him. They can't come to much harm together. Still, we'd better follow them and see what's up."

So they hurried along and presently came to the clearing where the wolf had been waiting.

"H'm," said Mrs. Wiggins, "more dogs, a lot of dogs. And they've all gone off together."

"Pretty big for dogs," said Eek, who was riding on Mrs. Wiggins's back.

The bear had been looking carefully at the tracks, and he put his nose down and smelt of them. "They're not dogs," he said quietly. "Wish they were. They're wolves. And if we want to see Jack and Charles again, we've got to hurry. Come along, and be ready for trouble." And he lumbered off rapidly on the trail the wolves had left behind them.

Only a few of the travellers had even heard of the existence of such animals as wolves, but it was no time for asking questions, and the bear looked so worried that they knew something really serious had happened. They swung along at a good round pace and by and by came to where the tracks disappeared into the cave. No one was in sight, but as they approached, a wolf walked out and stood facing them.

" Ah, good morning, friends," he said politely.

The animals stopped, all but Henrietta, who ruffled up her feathers and advanced upon the wolf, her head held low, ready to fly at him if he made a move in her direction. She looked really dangerous, though only a hen.

" I'll good-morning you, you disreputable varmint! " she clucked furiously. " Where's my husband? "

" My dear madam! " exclaimed the wolf.

" Really, I assure you it's unnecessary to take such a tone. Your husband and his friend are quite safe. There's just a little matter to be adjusted between us, and then — "

" Come, come," put in the bear, " not so many words, wolf. We want our friends." And he gave a low, deep, grumbling growl that made the wolf, for all his sarcastic grin, back a little way into the shelter of the cave mouth. " Come on; bring them out."

But the wolf shook his head. " Just a little formality to be observed first," he said. " Just hand those nice plump children over to us, and you shall have your friends at once."

His words seemed to drive Henrietta into a fury. " Formality, eh! " she screamed. " We'll teach you to put on airs with us! You let my husband out or we'll chew your heads off and make your moth-eaten hides up into a rug for Mr. Bean's kitchen! " And as the wolf started to laugh, she suddenly flew at him and, fixing her claws firmly into his shaggy head, pecked at his eyes until he howled with pain and had to roll on the ground to get rid of her. He was up in an instant, however, and darted at her with open jaws, all his sarcastic politeness forgotten. If he had caught her, it would have been the last of Henrietta, but the bear had stepped forward, and with a sudden blow of his enormous paw he sent the wolf sprawling over a log, where he lay for a moment before he picked himself up and limped back without a word into the cave.

" I guess that'll teach 'em! " said Henrietta. " Come on, animals. Let's go in and bring out Charles and Jack."

But the bear shook his head. " Not so fast," he said. " I know these wolves. Get ready for trouble; there's going to be plenty of it in a minute."

Almost before he had finished speaking, eight or nine long, lean bodies shot out of the cave opening, and in an instant the animals were fighting for their lives. The woods seemed to be full of wolves. They darted, wheeled, and snapped with their long, wicked jaws, seeking for a hold with which to pull their enemies down. At first the travellers were off their guard, and if the bear had not been ready, the rescue expedition would have come to an end right there. But, standing on his hind legs like a boxer, he knocked over two with a quick right and left at the first rush and, catching a third one by the tail in his big mouth, whirled him with a jerk of his head up into a pine-tree, where he hung, howling.

By this time the other animals had got into the fight. One of the wolves had caught hold of Everett and was dragging him towards the cave, but Cecil caught sight of him and, re-membering how he had persuaded Mrs. Wig-gins to jump out of the window, simply walked under the wolf and then gave a little jump, and the wolf yelped, let go, and ran off squeal-ing into the cave to pull the sharp quills out of his stomach. Each animal had a different method of fighting. Bill dashed about in short rushes like a small battering-ram, knocking over wolf after wolf, but not hurting them much. Mrs. Wiggins fought back to back with the bear, scooping up the wolves and tossing them high in the air. But she was such a kind-hearted animal that even in all the excitement and danger she tried not to wound them seriously with the points of her long, sharp horns. Uncle William reared and plunged, kicked and bit and trampled, and it was he who really turned the tide of battle, for when he turned round and lashed out with his hind legs, any wolf who was struck by those huge iron-shod hoofs was unlikely to take further interest in the fighting.

And presently the signal of recall was given, a long howl, and the wolves retreated into the cave, leaving three of their number helpless outside. The travellers took stock of their injuries. No one was hurt much, though the trampled snow was strewn with feathers and bits of fur. Ferdinand had sprained his beak slightly, and Mrs. Wiggins' tail was a little sore because one wolf had caught hold of it and tried to pull it off, and one of the mice was lost, having been shaken off the cow's back. But he turned up presently from a drift into which he had burrowed to be out of the way.

" My goodness! " said Mrs. Wiggins. " I didn't know fighting was so much fun! Strenuous, of course. But I don't know when I've enjoyed myself so much."

" It's fun when you win," said Uncle William. " But what do we do now? We can't follow up our victory, because the cave mouth is too small for us larger animals to get into."

At that moment the muzzle of the wolf leader appeared in the doorway. One eye was half closed as a result of Henrietta's attentions, but he could still grin.

" Well," he said, " now you've had your fun, I suppose you know who'll pay for it? "

" If you dare so much as touch a feather of my husband's head — " Henrietta began.

" Oh, we'll give you the feathers," said the wolf. " No use for them. But I trust it won't

164

come to that. Our offer still holds. Give us the children, and you can have your friends."

"I suppose you realize," said Ferdinand, "that we can stay here and starve you out?"

"Oh sure," admitted the wolf. "But you know we shan't starve until we've eaten you know whom." And he winked villainously. "Well," he added, "think it over. I'll be back for your answer in a little while." And he vanished.

Meanwhile inside the cave the two prisoners had been left undisturbed, although two guards were kept stationed just outside the door of their room. Jack lay down by the door, and Charles, who was getting hungry, wandered up and down, scratching now and then at the dirt floor in the hope of finding something to eat. Presently he uncovered half a dozen small black objects and, looking at them closely, discovered that they were large ants, which, after the manner of ants, were enjoying their winter's sleep. "H'm," said the rooster, "never liked ants much. Too spicy for my taste. But beggars can't be choosers." And with half a dozen quick pecks he swallowed the unsuspecting insects and then began scratching for more.

He had uncovered quite a colony of them and was making a meal of them when an idea struck him. He stopped eating and, catching hold of one of the ants by a leg, shook him roughly. " Hey," he shouted, " wake up! "

The ant stretched, yawned, then sat up and began washing his face with his forelegs.

" What's the idea? " he said crossly. " Can't you let a fellow sleep? "

" I beg your pardon," said Charles politely. " But it's a big piece of luck finding you here — "

" Luck for you or luck for me? " inquired the ant sarcastically.

" Both of us, I hope," said the rooster. " See here; how many of you ants are there in this ant-hill that I seem to have stumbled on? "

" Oh, about four thousand, last census," said the ant. " Four thousand soldiers, that is. We're the permanent garrison. I suppose there'd be as many more workers, but I don't know about that. — Say, is that all you waked me up for — to ask silly questions? What are you, a newspaper reporter or something? "

" No, no," said Charles. " The fact is, I've got a little military job I want done, and I'd like to hire about four thousand soldiers to do it. Of course I realize it means waking you all up in the winter when you want to sleep, but it isn't much of a job, really; won't take over an hour; and I'll pay well."

" Well, you've come to the right ant," said the other. " I'm captain of the Queen's Guard. But what's your idea of pay? "

" Honey," said Charles. " I've got about twenty pounds of honey that some bears brought in to pay for their seats at one of my lectures. I'm doing a lecture tour of the North, you see."

" No, I don't," said the ant. " I can't abide lectures. And why anybody should pay good honey to hear 'em — however, that's your business. H'm. Honey, eh? The boys haven't had any honey in a long time. I guess they wouldn't mind waking up for that. Well, that's O.K. Twenty pounds divided by four thousand soldiers — how much is that per ant? "

" Oh, figure it out afterwards," said Charles. " I'm in a hurry. My life's in danger; I haven't time to do arithmetic. How soon can you mobilize? "

" Have the whole army awake and in line in twenty minutes," said the captain. He looked about him. " Hey, Ed! " he shouted. " Why, where's Ed? And old Three Legs? See him anywhere? He lost the other three in a skirmish with some slave-hunting ants last fall. They were both sleeping right beside me."

Charles looked away and blushed slightly, for he was sure that both the captain's comrades were at that moment in his gizzard. But the ant didn't notice. " That's funny," he said. " Well, can't bother now." He seized a neighbouring sleeper by the feeler and shook him.

"Hey! Get up, Johnny! To arms, the Queen's Guard! Wake up, boys; here's a job for you." And he rushed about, kicking and punching and shaking his friends until half a dozen yawning, sleepy-eyed ants were grumbling and asking what was the matter.

"Run down to the citadel," said the captain, "and wake up General Formicularis and tell him to rouse the garrison and bring 'em up right away, all four regiments. Tell him to send through the barracks and turn 'em all out. Tell him there's good rich booty in it for everyone. Honey! That'll bring him."

The ants, old campaigners all, were by this time alert and wide awake, and they dashed down into the narrow passageways leading to the citadel. For a time there was no sound but a faint rustling underfoot, from where, deep down in the underground barracks and corridors and guard-rooms, the call to arms was being sounded.

Suddenly Charles cocked his ear towards

the door. " Isn't that Henrietta's voice? " he asked.

" Sounds like her," said Jack. " There's something going on outside. Perhaps they have come to rescue us."

" I thought I heard her voice," said Charles with what seemed to his friend a strange lack of enthusiasm. " She's angry at something."

" Probably at the wolves," said Jack.

" Yes, probably. But you know, Jack, I — I almost begin to like it here. It's quiet and peaceful and — "

" Nonsense! " said Jack. " You're afraid of Henrietta because she's angry. But she isn't angry at you. She wants to rescue you. Think how glad she'll be to see you — "

" She'll hide it pretty well," said Charles mournfully. " Oh yes, I suppose she'll be glad. But she'll give me an awful raking over for getting in such a mess. I shan't hear the last of it for months. — Ah, here we are! " he exclaimed as the head of a long procession of ant soldiers emerged from a small hole at his feet.

The soldiers came up at the double, and in a few minutes the entire army, four thousand strong, was spread out over the floor of the room, each of the regiments divided into companies with its captain at its head, and the general, a stout, puffy ant, a little in front, surrounded by his staff. Charles gave them a military salute with his right claw and then delivered a short address, telling them what he wanted them to do and ending with a stirring appeal to their patriotism, to the well-known fighting reputation of the famous First Division, which they comprised, and a promise of much honey.

Orders were quickly given. The first regiment, deployed as skirmishers, marched out along the roof of the cave; the others followed in columns of four. For perhaps five minutes after they had gone, there was silence, then a most terrific howling broke out among the wolves. "Hurray!" shouted Charles. "The attack has begun!" And he and Jack in their delight fell into each other's arms.

Outside the cave their friends, who had been holding a conference and trying to decide upon some method of rescue, were suddenly amazed to see a dozen wolves dash out of the dark opening, howling and snapping at their flanks and pawing madly at their heads. The wolves took no notice of their late enemies, but dashed off in different directions and were soon lost to sight. And before the watchers could recover from their surprise, out of the cave came Charles and Jack.

The animals rushed towards them and surrounded them. " What is it? " they exclaimed. " What did you do to them? They're gone, every last wolf. How in the world did you ever manage it? "

Charles puffed out his chest grandly. " Manage it? " he said. " Pooh! Nothing to it; nothing to it at all! Have any of you ever been bitten by an ant? "

" I have," said Bill. " I sat down in an ant-hill once by mistake, and my word! how those beasts can sting! "

" Well, that's all there was to it," said Charles. " I hired an ant army to attack them. Promised them honey. Somebody better go get that honey, by the way. And so here we are again, safe and sound. Ha! Ask old General Charles if you want to get anything done! I guess I showed those wolves a thing or two! I guess they won't try any tricks on this rooster again! "

But Henrietta pushed herself through his ring of admirers and caught him by the ear with her beak. " That's enough! " she said furiously. " You think you can cause me all this grief and then get away with it, do you? You think you can just stand around and tell how smart you are, eh? Well, I want a word with you, my lad! " And under the amused glances of his friends, she led him round behind a bush, from which he presently emerged, much crest-fallen. Nothing further was heard of his cleverness. Indeed he did not dare open his beak again in Henrietta's hearing for two days.

CHAPTER X
THE DASH FOR THE POLE

WORD of the brave fight that the travellers had put up had evidently gone round among the animals of the North, for they saw no more wolves after this, though they crossed the tracks of these animals every day. It grew colder and colder; the days were very short and the nights correspondingly long, so much of their travelling had to be done before sunrise and after sunset, by the wavering, drifting light of the aurora borealis. Soon they left the forest behind and travelled over endless snow plains, and the audiences of their lectures were composed mostly of reindeer. And at last they came to the polar sea.

"If I'm not mistaken," said Ferdinand, "this is about where we went adrift on the iceberg. Of course the sea is frozen over now, and the whaling ship must be frozen in the ice somewhere to the north of us. But we don't want to find the ship. My guess is that the crew, and probably our friends with them, will have reached Santa Claus's house long before this. That's at the north pole — straight north from here. See, here's a map of how we'll go." And he drew it in the snow. He made a mark and said: "That's where we are," and then he made another mark and said: "That's the north pole," and then he drew a straight line connecting them and said: "That's the route we take."

"H'm," said Mrs. Wiggins. "I don't see that that tells us much. I could have drawn that map myself."

"You're smarter than I thought you were,"

remarked Ferdinand, and Mrs. Wiggins didn't know whether to be angry or not. But the other animals all agreed that that was the only course to take, so they set out due north over the frozen sea.

And in two days they heard news of their friends. Just before dusk — which came at two in the afternoon — Ferdinand, who had gone for a short flight to stretch his wings, which were apt to get a little stiff with disuse when he rode on Bill's head and didn't use them all day, spied a black speck in the northern sky. It grew larger and larger, and presently he saw that it was a huge eagle. Ferdinand climbed to meet him, since he knew that only a very hungry eagle will condescend to eat a crow. And soon they were flying side by side.

" Hail, crow," said the eagle. " Whither away so far from home? " Eagles always speak in very high-flown language and are very touchy of their dignity, because they are the national bird.

"Good evening, your honour," said Ferdinand. "I'm with a party who have come to rescue a number of friends. They were captured by the crew of a whaling ship, and the last we heard of them, they were bound for the pole to visit Santa Claus. Have you seen anything of them? "

"These eyes beheld them only yesterday," said the eagle over his shoulder, for he was flying much faster than Ferdinand, who had a hard time to keep up.

"Hey! " said the crow. "What's that? Would you slow up a little and circle around a bit? It's very important to me."

The eagle shrugged his shoulders. "Is a crow's business as important as an eagle's? " he demanded. "And he the messenger of Santa Claus? I have no time for your petty affairs, crow. And yet — " He paused in his flight, banked, and soared in a wide circle. "Perchance at this juncture even the aid of the lowly crow is not to be despised. So listen and heed well, for I have little time to spare.

Things have gone very ill with my master since the arrival of those seafaring men and their pets — "

" They're there, then? " interrupted Ferdinand.

" I bade you *listen,*" said the eagle sharply. " Did I not speak of their arrival? You are wasting with your idle words time that is far more precious than your own — more precious even than mine, for it is the time of my master, Santa Claus, and it lacks but a short space of time to Christmas." He said considerably more about wasting time, but Ferdinand had sense enough not to point out that if time was being wasted, it was not he who was wasting it. And presently the eagle went on.

" You have left me little time to inform you how affairs stand, and indeed it is a long story. You are eager, I take it, to rescue your friends and return them to the country of their birth. In this you may be assured of my help — for I shall return in a week — and of the help of others whose acquaintance you will soon make. But those sailors must also be persuaded to return to their pursuit of whales, and this will be no easy matter. It is a problem on which we will consult together upon my return. Farewell, crow, and convey to that excellent pig, your friend, my kindest remembrances."

" But," said Ferdinand hastily, as the eagle began to flap his huge wings, " just what *is* the matter? You haven't told — "

" He is indeed a most talented member of the porcine race," went on the eagle. " Never to my knowledge have I been paid so delicate and tactful a compliment as in the poem which he wrote about me. Let me see; how did it go?

O eagle, mightiest of all living things,
Nor Death nor Destiny spreads stronger wings.
Thy claws of brass, thy beak of burnished steel,
Make malefactor pigs in terror squeal.

And so on. Very beautiful words. Request him to sing it for you."

" Yes, I will; but you haven't — " Ferdinand began. The eagle by this time, however, was under way. " Good-bye," he shouted, and drew away from the disappointed crow at a speed which made pursuit useless.

" Well, he was a lot of help," grumbled Ferdinand as he swooped earthward. " However, we know where they are, and Freddy's all right. That's something."

The animals had watched the meeting with the eagle with great interest and continued the day's march in the highest spirits when they learned that they were really within so short a distance of their friends. But a day's flight to an eagle may be a week's hard going for an animal, and it was several days before there was any indication that they were nearing the pole. Meanwhile they racked their brains to guess what the eagle had meant when he had hinted that things were not all as they should be at Santa Claus's house. Indeed, they had several quarrels about it, some holding one view, some another, until it was decided that the only sensible plan was to give up talking and speculating about it until they got there.

On the second day after meeting the eagle they climbed up through a low range of ice hills, and Ferdinand said that they were again on land, though it made no difference to them, since both earth and water were frozen, and covered with ice and snow. North from the hills stretched an empty, snowy plain, but they had not gone far over this when they came to something very strange: a gate.

It was a very neat gate, with strong posts set solidly into the snow, and made of pickets freshly painted green, so that it could be seen for a long distance. And tacked to one side of it was a piece of plank with the following legend painted on it:

KEEP OUT
This means YOU! !
By order of the Board

The animals gathered round it. " What are we to keep out *of?* " they asked each other.

" It looks so silly, without any fence," said Mrs. Wiggins. " I never heard of such a thing. A gate without a fence is like a roof without any barn under it."

" And what's the board? " asked Jack.

" The only board is the one the sign's painted on," said Ferdinand. " I expect that's what it means."

" Well, I don't take any orders from any old board," said Bill. And he went back a little way and put his head down and ran at the sign and butted it flat on the snow.

So the animals went on, and in an hour or two they came to another sign.

TRESPASSERS WILL BE PROSECUTED
S. C., Inc.
Hooker, G. M.

Again the animals were puzzled, but Uncle William said: " There are signs like that on

" What are we to keep out of? "

some of the farms down our way. I think trespassers are people that shoot and fish. And
prosecuting is what the farmer does to them if
he catches them."

"Well, we haven't got guns or fish-poles,"
said Jack, "and if we had, there's nothing to use them on. I wonder who S. C.,
Inc., is."

"Probably the farmer," said the horse.
"And Hooker, G. M., is his address. Like the
letters Mrs. Bean sends to her sister, addressed: Elizabeth, N. J., you know."

"But there isn't any state called G. M.,"
said Ferdinand. "N. J. is New Jersey, but who
ever heard —"

"Well, we're in Canada," interrupted Cecil.
"Perhaps that's the state of Canada we're in."

"Oh, come on," said the bear. "All these
signs mean we're getting somewhere, at least."
And he started on.

"I don't want to be prosecuted," said
Mrs. Wiggins doubtfully. But she followed the
others as they trailed on past the sign.

They were getting so near the pole now that they had no sunlight at all to travel by. They were in the region where the sun shines day and night all summer long, but where in winter it never lifts its bright head above the horizon. The continuous darkness made the bear even more sleepy, so that he had to have Cecil ride on his back and jump up and down occasionally when he began to get too drowsy. And they could only tell what time of day it was by the position of the stars.

Just after passing the second sign they noticed a glow on the northern horizon which was neither stars nor northern lights, and as they went on, the glow spread and began to twinkle with little points of light. More and more sparkling lights appeared, and in a little while they saw what it was — a long hedge of Christmas-trees, all trimmed with tinsel streamers and gold and silver stars and shiny blue and green and red balls and lighted up with hundreds and thousands of little candles.

And behind the hedge they could just make out the gleaming walls and pinnacles and towers and turrets of a tremendous ice palace.

They gave a cheer and hurried forward. They pushed through the hedge and saw before them a high gateway in a wall of ice. High above them in the wall were windows in which lights twinkled. Here they hesitated for a moment, and Ferdinand looked round for the door-bell, but Uncle William said: " The gate's ajar. It must be all right to go in." He pushed with his shoulder, and the gate swung open.

They followed him a little doubtfully into a big courtyard, tastefully planted with holly bushes, interspersed with Christmas-trees in tubs, and with a frozen fountain in the middle. They were wondering what they should do next when they heard someone singing. The voice was a light pleasing tenor; it had a familiar ring to their ears. And these were the words:

186

O Pole, O Pole, O glorious Pole!
   To you I sing this song,
Where bedtime comes but once a year,
   Since the nights are six months long.

Yes, the nights are six months long, my dears,
   And the days are the same, you see,
So breakfast and supper each last a week,
   And dinner sometimes three.

Then there's tea and lunch, and we sometimes munch
   Occasional snacks between —
Such mountains of candies and cakes and pies
   Have never before been seen.

Let the wild winds howl about the Pole,
   Let the snow-flakes swirl and swoop;
We're snug and warm and safe from harm
   And they're bringing in the soup.

We'll sit at the table as long as we're able,
   We'll rise and stretch, and then,
Since there's nothing to do but gobble and chew,
   We'll sit right down again.

We'll tuck our napkins under our chins
   To keep our waistcoats neat,
And then we'll eat and eat and eat
   And eat and eat and eat.

187

" Nobody but a greedy pig would sing a song like that," muttered Ferdinand disgustedly.

" It's piggish, all right," said Jack, " but I'm glad to hear that voice." And he shouted: " Freddy! " and all the others shouted with him.

A small round startled face appeared at one of the upper windows and vanished again, and in a few moments a door was flung open and Freddy himself came dashing out. " Ferdinand! " he shouted. " You brought 'em! Good old Ferdy! And Jack! And Mrs. Wiggins! Gosh, but I'm glad to see you! And Uncle William and Charles and Henrietta, and even the mice! Golly, this is *great!* " He rushed round hugging them one after the other. " And these two children! Now where in the world did you pick them up? — But come in, come in! Mustn't stay out in the cold, and we've a lot to say to each other."

He led them into a large hall, at the far end

188

of which was a fireplace as big as a barn-door, in which huge logs were burning brightly. "Take off your things and sit down," said Freddy, throwing off the handsome fur coat he had been wearing.

"My goodness, Freddy, you're fat as butter," said Mrs. Wiggins.

Freddy had indeed grown dreadfully stout. He was almost perfectly round, and his cheeks were so fat that his eyes were almost invisible. He looked slightly displeased at the cow's remark, but then he smiled and his eyes disappeared entirely. "High living," he explained. "We live well here on the top of the world."

As they approached the fire, a big man with a bushy white beard and sharp black eyes, twinkling with fun and kindliness, rose from a deep chair and came towards them. He had on a fur-trimmed red coat, belted at the waist, and green trousers tucked into high black boots, and there were bells at his wrists and knees that jingled when he moved.

The animals stopped self-consciously. They knew it was no one but Santa Claus himself.

" He looks enough like Mr. Bean to be his brother! " said Mrs. Wiggins.

" Ssssh! " Freddy warned her. " He understands our talk."

But Santa Claus had heard the remark, and he smiled. " I know of your Mr. Bean," he said. " He is a fine man; I am proud to resemble him in any way."

Then Freddy presented his friends, and Santa Claus shook hands warmly with each of them. When he came to the bear, " And this," the pig said, " is — er — ah — hrrumph — "

" I beg your pardon," said the saint. " I didn't catch your name."

The bear shifted awkwardly from one foot to another and blushed — at least he blushed inside, but it couldn't be seen through his fur. " I — er — I — Well, I haven't any name," he said finally.

" No name? " said Santa Claus. " Well,

now, how did that happen? You're the first animal I ever knew who hadn't one."

The bear hesitated a moment; then he said: " Well, sir, I really have got a name, but I never liked it, so I never used it. It's — no, I can't say it. It's so silly."

" H'm," said Santa Claus thoughtfully. " If you don't like your name, there's no reason why you shouldn't change it. Isn't there any name you like? "

The bear brightened. " Really? " he asked. " I always thought you had to keep your name, whether you liked it or not. But if you say so — "

" I do," said Santa Claus.

" Well, then, the name I choose is Peter," said the bear.

" That's a fine name," said Santa Claus. " I'm glad to make your acquaintance, Peter. And now, animals, come up round the fire and make yourselves comfortable. You must be cold after such a long trip. Get warm first, and then Freddy will show you your rooms and you can wash up, and then we'll have some supper."

" There's one thing we'd like to ask you, sir," said Ferdinand, and he repeated what the eagle had told him. " Is it true that these sailors have caused trouble? "

A worried look came into the saint's eyes. " Trouble? " he said. " Oh, I wouldn't say that. They've changed things certainly. They — "

He stopped, for at that moment a door flew open and a man came into the room — a tall thin man, with drooping black moustaches and hard, sharp black eyes. He had sea boots on, and a red sash about his waist, in which a pistol was stuck. " Ah, Mr. Claus," he said in a harsh voice, " talkin' to the animals again, eh? I thought I heard you." He swept a contemptuous glance over the group about the fire. " Well, I'm sorry to disturb you, but there's this here matter of the workmen in the mechanical-toy department; they don't seem to want to adopt the suggestions of Mr. Pomeroy, and we think you'd better talk to 'em. Then the New York *Times* just came in on the last mail, and there's an editorial there about you we think you should answer. We've got the answer all drafted, but we want your signature."

Santa Claus got up wearily. " All right, all right; I'll come," he said. Then turning to his new guests, " Freddy will entertain you until I'm at liberty," he said. " And he can answer the question you just asked me." He stooped suddenly and caught up Ella and swung her to his shoulder, then held out a hand to Everett. " You children come along with me," he said.

The children giggled delightedly, but the man with the harsh voice said: " Surely, Mr. Claus, you don't intend to bring these children to a business conference? They'll only be in the way. They — "

" Surely I do," boomed Santa Claus in his deep bass voice. " This business is run for children and don't you forget it. When you leave the children out, you leave Santa Claus out, Mr. Hooker. Let's have that perfectly clear."

Hooker shrugged and turned on his heel, and before he followed him, Santa Claus paused and whispered to the children: " Don't mind him. He isn't as unpleasant as he tries to make out. And, anyway, I'll tell you stories all the time he's talking." And the door closed behind them.

CHAPTER XI
SANTA AND THE SAILORS

The animals, who had stood up politely when Santa Claus left the room, gathered again round the fire and began asking Freddy questions. The pig settled back comfortably in his chair.

" Well, I'll tell you all about it," he said. " But don't sit on the floor. What are all these chairs for? "

" Animals don't use chairs," said Uncle William. " Chairs are for human beings. When I was with the circus, one of my acts had to be done sitting in a chair, and I was never so uncomfortable in my life."

" Once you get used to 'em," said Freddy, " you'll never go back to the floor. Try that big one there, Mrs. Wiggins." The cow looked at it doubtfully. " Don't be afraid," he continued. " All this furniture is made in Santa Claus's workshop; it's none of your flimsy factory-made stuff that falls apart if you breathe on it."

So Mrs. Wiggins sat down gingerly; then, as nothing happened, leaned back with a sigh. " My goodness, it *is* comfortable as all get-out," she said.

" Of course it is. — Well, I'll get on with my story. You know what happened up to the time that Ferdinand left us. After that we sailed north for a time, and then the ice-pack closed in on the ship, so we left it and went on across the ice. We reached here without any trouble, except for Jinx's head; he had a row with a polar bear. Jinx said something fresh to the bear — you know how Jinx is — and the bear hit him a clip with his paw and took all the hair off Jinx's head — snatched

196

him bald-headed. It'll grow again all right, Santa Claus says, but he certainly does look funny."

" But where *is* Jinx? " asked Jack. " And all the rest of them? Why don't they come say hello to us? "

" Yes," said Ferdinand. " After all, we did come to rescue you animals. And now there's nobody but you to welcome us."

" Oh, I forgot to tell you — they're all out skiing. They'll be back by dinner-time. All except Jinx. He spends all his time down in the gymnasium. We'll go down in a few minutes and find him. — Well, as I was saying, when we got here, Santa Claus was kindness itself. He gave a big dinner-party for us that night, and the next day showed us over his whole place. That's how the trouble started. While he was showing us the work-rooms where the toys are made, and explaining how he finds out what children want and sees that they get the right toys in their stockings and on their Christmas-trees, I heard Mr. Pomeroy, the mate of the ship, say to the captain: 'This place wants systematizing, Mr. Hooker.'

" 'You're right, as you nearly always are, Mr. Pomeroy,' said the captain. 'Efficiency, that's what's needed. I never see a place run as inefficient as this is.'

" They went on talking in the same way, and I didn't think much about it then; but next day they came into this room and asked if they could talk to Santa Claus about his business — said they had some suggestions to make. Santa Claus said he was always glad to get suggestions, and then they began. I was here and heard all of it. The captain said that they had been greatly interested in going over the plant, but that both he and his friends had been surprised and even alarmed at the old-fashioned way in which things were run.

" 'Why, what's the matter with them?' asked Santa.

" 'Pretty near everything,' said Hooker solemnly, and Mr. Pomeroy nodded gloomily. 'Yes, sir,' the captain went on, 'our expert opinion is that in five years, if you keep on, runnin' like this, you'll have to close down.'

" ' Suppose you tell me exactly what you think is wrong,' said Santa.

" ' Well, sir,' said the captain, ' things in America have changed a good deal in the past twenty-five years. Your methods of manufacture and distribution is as out of date as your grandmother's lace cap — with all due respect. Take the matter of chimneys. You take the toys down the chimney Christmas Eve. You've always done it that way, and you're still doing it that way, in spite of the fact that in modern houses the chimney doesn't go down to a fireplace where the children hang up their stockings — it goes straight down to the furnace in the cellar. And in big apartment houses you can't get to some of the children at all.'

" ' We have our ways of getting round that,' said Santa Claus.

" ' Sure you do,' said the captain. ' But it's a lot of trouble. No, sir, Mr. Claus, that's only one thing, and there's dozens. Suppose, for instance, you had a hundred per cent efficient factory here; what good is that if you can't get rid of your product? What are you doing to make the children of America toy-conscious? Where in this great land of ours will you find another firm which doesn't spend one penny for advertising? No advertising appropriation *at all!* Think of it, Mr. Pomeroy! '

" ' I am,' said the mate with a groan. ' It's suicidal, Mr. Hooker; that's what it is: suicidal! '

" Santa Claus tried to say something, but the captain went right on. ' Take the matter of publicity, now, Mr. Claus. I admit you get a lot of free publicity every year at Christmas-time. Your picture's in all the magazines. Yes, but it's all in other people's advertisements. And you're wearin' the same old suit and drivin' the same old reindeer you were drivin' when my dear old grandpa was a dirty-faced kid. You're too far away, Mr. Claus; you ain't got your finger on the pulse of the nation.'

" Well, there was a lot more of it, and every time Santa Claus tried to say something, one or other of 'em would interrupt him and go on. And then they made what they called their proposition to him. They would come in and reorganize his business for him. It wouldn't cost him a cent, they said — ' And in two months, Mr. Claus,' said the mate, ' you won't know the place.'

" It surprised us all a lot when we found out he had agreed to do it. I think he did it partly because he was tired of hearing them talk, and partly because they really thought they were doing him a favour. He's very kind-hearted, and he thought their feelings would be hurt if he wouldn't let them help him. So what they did was this: they organized a company: Santa Claus, Incorporated — "

" Why," exclaimed Jack, " that's what the ' S. C., Inc.,' meant on the sign we saw."

" Yes," said Freddy. " It was incorporated just like our Barnyard Tours at home."

" But it said: ' Hooker, G. M.,' on the sign,

too," said Charles. " What did that mean? And that other sign that said: ' By order of the Board ' ? "

" ' Hooker, G. M.,' means ' Hooker, General Manager,' " said Freddy. " And the Board is the Board of Governors. That consists of Santa Claus and the captain and Mr. Pomeroy and Mr. Bashwater. He was the chief harpooner of the whaling ship, and he's now the efficiency expert."

" Good grief! " exclaimed Mrs. Wiggins. " What a lot of big words about nothing! It's all a pack of nonsense, if you ask me."

" That's what we all think," said Freddy. " But Santa Claus is worried about it. They're changing everything, and he doesn't know what to do. We've got to help him get rid of them."

" Just what have they done? " asked Ferdinand.

" Well, they put all those signs round, warning people away. Of course that doesn't matter, because nobody pays any attention to them. But they've started an eight-hour day in the workshops — everybody has to be there at eight and work until five, with an hour out for lunch. You see, these people that make the toys come from all over the United States. They're people who used to work in offices and factories, and who have got too old, or are not well enough, to work so hard. When Santa Claus hears about anybody like that, he sends for him and brings him up here. He used to let these people work when they wanted to. If they wanted to stop for a while and play games or read or rest, why, they just did it, and then by and by went back and worked some more. But that's all changed now, and they don't like it very much. That kind of hard work is just the thing Santa Claus wanted to help them to get away from.

" Then the people in the workshops used to make the toys any way they wanted to. If they wanted to paint a toy rabbit pink and give him a tail like a squirrel's, they did it. But now each kind of toy has to be made in just one way, and one workman cuts it out, and the next paints the body and passes it on to the third, who paints in the eyes, and so on. Each workmen does just one thing. Santa didn't like it, but Mr. Bashwater said that it was mass production, whatever that means. He said that that was how Mr. Henry Ford managed to turn out so many automobiles. But Santa Claus said: 'Mr. Henry Ford makes toys for grown-ups. Every grown-up likes to have his toys just like every other grown-up's. But children like their toys different.' "

" That's so," put in Bill. " When Mrs. Bean got that sewing-machine, I heard her tell the man who sold it to her that she wanted it just like the one Mrs. Swazy had."

" You'd think she'd want it a little different, wouldn't you? " said Mrs. Wiggins.

" People are funny," said Uncle William.

Freddy told them some more about the changes that the sailors were making, and then took them upstairs. " This is my room," he said, throwing open a door. It was a bright and cozy little room. The furniture was painted bright blue with red trimmings, and the chintz window-curtains showed a pattern of small red pigs playing tag in a blue clover field, and over the fireplace was a painting of three very handsome pigs with blue silk bows around their necks, sitting in a row on a sofa and looking very self-conscious, as anyone does when he is having his picture painted.

" You don't mean to say you sleep in that bed? " said Bill.

" Sure, I do," replied the pig. " You don't know how comfortable it is until you've tried it. Did you ever sleep in one? "

" Me? " exclaimed the goat disgustedly. " I should say not! "

" Well," said Freddy, " I used to think that human beings were softies because they didn't sleep on bare boards with a little straw, the way most animals do. But I've changed my mind. Why shouldn't we be as comfortable as we can? You wait till you've tried that nice soft bed in your room, Bill."

The goat snorted and was about to make a sarcastic reply, when Cecil, who had been looking out of the window, shouted: " Oh, look! There come the others! "

Sure enough, through an opening in the Christmas-tree hedge shot a fur-muffled figure on skis, to be followed by another and then another. The first two, leaning sideways, made a graceful turn and brought up in a flurry of snow close to the palace wall, but the third, who seemed very large and clumsy, turned too sharply and went head over heels in a double somersault, while the skis flew high in the air. The fur cap had fallen off, revealing the kind face and mild brown eyes of Mrs. Wogus, who gazed about with a somewhat dazed and surprised look, and then, catching sight of the grins on the faces of her companions, broke into a loud laugh.

Freddy threw up the window and called out the news to them, and they tumbled upstairs and greeted their friends with delight. They made a great hubbub with their laughter and questions and answers; and Mrs. Wogus insisted on kissing all the new-comers, which none of them liked very much, for she had a very large wet nose anyway, and now her face was covered with melting snow. The mice were drenched and shivering after she had kissed them, and Freddy had to take them into the bathroom and give them a rub-down with a towel so they wouldn't catch cold.

Then he showed them all their rooms. Each one had furniture just the right size for the animal who was to use it. The mice shared a room together, and it looked like a room in a doll house, with its three tiny beds covered with little patchwork quilts, the small rocking-chairs, and the framed photograph of an Edam cheese over the mantel. Each room had its private bath, and although some of them were on different sides of the palace, Freddy assured them that they all had a southern exposure. " It's the only house in the world," he said, " in which all the rooms face south."

It took some time for the animals to

understand this. " Don't be silly, Freddy," said Mrs. Wiggins. " How can windows on all sides of a house face in the same direction? "

" Because this house is built on the north pole. There isn't any direction but south here."

" But suppose I leave here and want to go west," said Charles.

" You can't," said Freddy. " Because any direction you go from here is straight towards the south pole."

The cow thought a minute. " Yes, I see that," she said. " But it seems funny to me. If we start somewhere, and both go in the same direction, we're together, aren't we? "

Freddy agreed that this must be so.

" Well, then, if I start out of the back door of this house, and you start out of the front door, and Hank starts out of the side door, we're all going in the same direction. And yet we aren't going together at all, and the farther we go, the farther apart we are."

" Yes," said Freddy, " but if we keep on long enough, we'll all meet in the same place, the south pole, so we must be *really* getting nearer together all the time." And he went on with a long explanation, which interested him so much that he never noticed that the others had gradually left the room. Then he looked up and saw that there was no one with him. " Well, well," he sighed, " that's what it is to be a poet." And he went back to his own room, sat down at the little writing-desk by the window, on the wall above which were pinned various sets of verses he was working on, and started another poem. He wrote:

> Oh east is east, and west is west,
> And never the twain shall meet —

Then he stopped and frowned. " Reminiscent, somehow," he muttered: " Wonder if it's too metaphysical. It's darned good, though." He went on.

> Until they come to the end of the earth,
> To Santa Claus' retreat.

He stopped again. " Oh, yes, I remember," he said, and grinned. " It'll make Kipling pretty sore — gives him the lie direct." Then he continued.

Where east is south, and west is south
    And north is south also;
Where all directions are the same,
    Whichever way you go.

" Hey, Freddy," came Hank's voice from the hall. " We're going down to the gym."

Freddy sighed, put in a comma and two exclamation points, then after pinning the paper up beside the others, hurried downstairs to the gymnasium, through the glass door of which the new arrivals were peering with many nudgings and suppressed giggles. For inside, Jinx, as yet unaware of their gaze, was looking at himself in a long mirror. Beside him was a small jar of ointment, and every now and then he would scoop a little out on his paw and rub it carefully into the bald spot on the top of his head, and then he would turn and twist his neck in the effort to see better. He looked very discontented with his appearance while doing

210

this, but pretty soon he backed away from the glass a little and, keeping his chin up so he couldn't see the bald spot, tried the effect of various expressions. He tried looking dignified, and he tried smiling graciously, and he tried looking nonchalant, and superior, and arch, and imposing, and unconcerned in a thunderstorm. But he was so pleased with all these expressions that gradually they all came to be one expression, and whatever he tried he just succeeded in smirking in a self-satisfied way. And at that moment the pressure against the gymnasium door, against which all the animals were pushing in order to see, got so strong that it flew suddenly open, and they all fell in on the floor.

At the crash Jinx jumped three feet in the air, and his tail got as big as a whisk broom, but when he saw who it was, he was so delighted that he forgot to be angry, and when he had greeted them all, he showed them over the gymnasium.

" I spend most of my time here," he said.

" I don't care much for outdoor sports this winter."

" What do you do, mostly? " asked Jack.

" Oh, I've been doing some high trapeze work," replied the cat. " It's said to be rather dangerous — jumping from trapeze to trapeze in mid air, and so on — but, goodness, what of that! I always say, what's life without a little spice of danger — "

" Show us some of your stunts," said Bill.

" Eh? " said Jinx. " Oh yes, I will some time. Let me show you what Santa Claus gave me yesterday." And he brought out a mechanical mouse, which he wound up and set on the floor, and it ran about just like a real one. " I practise hunting with it. See? " He made a pounce and caught the toy between his fore-paws.

But at this exhibition Cousin Augustus shuddered, covering his eyes with his paw, and the three other mice squeaked violently.

Jinx turned and looked at them. " Hey! " he said. " What's the matter? Why good gosh, that doesn't mean anything! Any more than when children play war, with toy swords and pistols, it means they're going to shoot each other. Don't be so silly, mice."

But the mice didn't like it and said so. " Suppose we came in here some time and you got us mixed up," said Eeny. " Where'd we be then? " So Jinx had to apologize and put the mechanical mouse away.

Pretty soon they all went down to supper. The animals all sat at one end of the huge banquet hall at small tables, four at a table according to size. The horses and cows were together, and in front of them were big bowls containing oats, and a big heap of fragrant hay in the centre of the table. At another table were the two dogs and the cat and the pig, and even the mice had a tiny table, which fairly groaned under the weight of an assortment of cheeses — Cousin Augustus counted fourteen kinds. The animals were a little nervous at first about eating at a table, since none of them were used to it, but of course they didn't have to use knives and forks, and they got on pretty well, though they didn't know what to do with the napkins they found at their places. Mrs. Wiggins thought you were supposed to eat them, and she had actually started to chew hers, when her sister stopped her and explained what they were for. Then she said: " Good gracious, I hope I can eat my supper without getting it all over my chin! Fine manners Santa Claus must think we have, to give us these things! "

After supper they went down to a room that was even bigger than the banquet hall. It was called the Present Room, and each of them was given a present, because at Santa Claus's house it was Christmas all the time, so everybody gets a present every day. The presents were very nice. Freddy got a ten-pound box of candied fruit, and Jinx got a red and white striped gymnasium suit, and Mrs. Wogus got a book on skiing, and Hank, who was learning to read, got a copy of *Black Beauty*, and Robert got a collar with his name on it in rhinestones, and so on. Even the mice each got a tiny wristwatch, and Ella got a big doll, and Everett got an electric train.

Besides the presents that were given to them, there were hundreds and thousands of toys and books and doll houses and presents of all kinds in the Present Room, and they could play with any they wanted to. They spent a very happy evening there, but it had been a busy day, and by nine o'clock they were all tucked up in bed and the lights were out — all except Freddy's. He was sitting at his desk, and in front of him was a sheet of paper on which was written in big capitals: " ODE TO SANTA CLAUS." And under it was written: " O Santa Claus — " And under that on the paper was Freddy's head, for when he had got that far in the poem, he had fallen asleep.

CHAPTER XII
IN THE POLAR PALACE

THERE were so many pleasant things to do in Santa Claus's palace that it seemed to the animals that they had hardly finished breakfast before it was time to go to bed. Outdoors they skated and ski'd and tobogganed, and when they slid down hill, there were always some of Santa Claus's reindeer who were glad to pull them up to the top of the hill in exchange for a ride down. They built magnificent snow forts and had pitched battles: animals against sailors. The animals couldn't throw snowballs so straight as the sailors, but they were better strategists; that is, they didn't just give a loud shout and charge the enemy; they retreated and avoided battle until the enemy was in a bad position. Some of these battles lasted all day. Near the palace there was a little depression in the snow surrounded by low ice cliffs, and it was here almost always that the sailors met defeat. They couldn't seem to learn how it was done. Yet it was very simple. As soon as the battle started near the palace, Freddy would lead half the animal army quietly away and station them on the top of these cliffs. Then the rest of the animals would pretend to run away, and the sailors would follow them, shouting and cheering, with Hooker in the lead, waving a wooden sword and yelling: " Forward, my hearties! On to victory! Hew them down! Let not a man escape! " and so on. He loved to lead these charges.

The retreating animals would rush helter-skelter down into the depression in the snow and up the other side, the sailors hot on their heels. But as soon as the animals had reached the top of the cliffs, they would turn and begin heaving down masses of snow on the sailors, and the other animals, who had remained hidden until then, would start rolling down huge snowballs that they had prepared, and pretty soon the sailors would be completely buried in snow, and the animals would have to come down and dig them out.

And then they'd all trudge home together to supper, tired and happy, Mr. Hooker riding on the back of Uncle William or Mrs. Wiggins, and shouting to his mate: " That was a fine fight, Mr. Pomeroy. We'd 'a won, too, if there hadn't been so much snow come tumblin' down on us. Well, we'll try it again tomorrow."

Sometimes they stayed indoors and played games in the Present Room, or dressed up and did charades, or worked the electric railroads, or had yacht-races in the swimming-pool. There was every kind of game or toy you could think of in the Present Room, so that they

could do something different every day for a
year if they wanted to. They played with Ella
and Everett too. Everett drilled them like soldiers, and Ella had them sit on benches and
pretended to teach school. When they were
bad and shuffled their feet and whispered and
pinched each other, she spanked them. She
knew how to spank, too, because she had been
spanked so many times herself by Kate. But
of course she didn't spank very hard. It was
funny to see her trying to spank Mrs. Wiggins
or Hank. Sometimes she played school with
the sailors, and they really learned a good deal,
for their grammar wasn't very good, and Ella
had learned a lot of grammar from Pete.

"What is the subject of the sentence ' I saw
the cat,' Mr. Pomeroy? " she would ask.

"Hey, Mr. Hooker," the mate would mut-
ter behind his hand, " give me a little help, will
you? "

The captain would look very virtuous.
"Can't do it, Mr. Pomeroy," he would answer
in a hoarse whisper. " 'Tain't fair. If you don't

know, say so." Mr. Hooker had no more idea what the answer was than the mate did.

Then Mr. Bashwater, the harpooner, who knew the answers to practically every question because he had had a college education, would whisper: " ' I ' is the answer."

And Mr. Pomeroy would think that Mr. Bashwater was making fun of him and would turn round, forgetting he was in school, and say angrily: " What d'ye mean — ' I is the answer ' ! You trying to be funny? You can't say: ' I is.' It's ' I am.' "

" I mean ' I ' is the subject," Mr. Bashwater would try to explain, but that would only make it worse, and it would end by both Mr. Bashwater and Mr. Pomeroy being sent to stand in the corner with their faces to the wall, for quarrelling.

The animals and the sailors were really very fond of one another, and so although the animals were trying as hard as they could to think of some way of getting the sailors to go away and let Santa Claus alone, they wanted to do it without hurting them or making them unhappy. They talked about it a good deal among themselves.

One day Jack was out watching Mr. Bashwater practising throwing his harpoon at a snow man to keep his hand in. The captain and the mate and the boatswain, a very untidy sailor named Joel, were looking on, applauding the good shots and groaning at the bad ones, and sometimes pretending that the snow man was really a whale. " Thar she blows! " Joel would shout. " Two p'ints off the port bow! " And Mr. Pomeroy would squint under the flat of his hand and sing out: " Eighty barrels, if she's a pint! " meaning that they would get that much oil from the whale. And then Mr. Bashwater would throw the harpoon and bellow: " All aboard for a Nantucket sleighride! " which is a term whalers use for being towed by a whale to which they have made fast.

" I tell you what, Mr. Pomeroy," said the captain; " I sometimes get home-sick for the old ship. Yes, sir, home-sick ain't the word for what I feel sometimes, thinkin' o' them moon-lit nights with the canvas a creakin' and the riggin' a singin' in the wind and the black water a foamin' past."

" And them other nights, Mr. Hooker," replied the mate, " with the fire from the try works lightin' up the sea around us, and the blubber a boilin' and a sputterin' in the kettles, and the thick oily smoke a chokin' us so we can't hardly breathe."

" Ain't no sweeter smell than whale-oil," put in the harpooner. " But where all the whales is gone to I dunno."

" Ah, that's just it," said Hooker, thoughtfully pulling his long black moustache. " If I thought we'd have any luck, I wouldn't stay here another day. Still an' all, it's a good life — easier'n shipboard — and once this business is put on a real efficiency basis — "

" Yes," said Mr. Bashwater as he hurled his harpoon again at the snow man, " and the men is contented, ain't they, Joel? "

" Ay, that they are," said the boatswain.

" Happy as larks, they are. And why, sir? Well, if you ask me — "

" We didn't ask you, Joel," said Mr. Hooker quietly. " Don't forget that."

" No, sir, now I come to think, you didn't. But I'll tell you anyway. They're happy because they get lots to eat and presents every day, and because they can lie abed o' mornin's, but mostly on account o' the ice cream."

" The ice cream! " exclaimed the mate.

" Ay, sir. Y' see, our cookie is a good cook; I ain't breathin' a whisper against him. But he ain't no hand with a freezer; you know it yourself, sir. While Mr. Claus's ice cream — well, sir, I never tasted nothin' like it. It's grand, and that's the gospel truth."

Jack did not wait to hear any more, but went up into the Present Room, where his friends were playing games. He told them what Joel had said. " And," he added, " if we could do something to the ice cream so it wouldn't be so good, maybe the sailors would get homesick, and then they would leave of their own accord."

The animals didn't think it was a very bright idea, but as it was the only one they had, they decided to try it out. Freddy, who spent a good deal of time in the kitchen and could come and go there without being noticed, went downstairs and presently returned with the inside part of the freezer under his fur coat. They put it on Mrs. Wiggins's left horn, and after several tries she managed to punch a hole through it. Then Freddy took it back. And that day at dinner the ice cream was so salty that no one could eat it.

The animals were greatly pleased when they looked down the long dining-room and saw the sailors waving their arms angrily and beating on the table with their spoons and heard the shouts of anger. " That'll fix 'em," said Freddy. " If we can just keep them good and discontented, the captain'll have to take them back to the ship." But unfortunately for their plot, Santa Claus, having found out the cause of the trouble, had an enormous bowl of caramel custard brought in to take the place of the ice cream. The animals, knowing that the ice cream would be bad, had all said they didn't want any dessert, so of course the caramel custard wasn't passed to them, and the sailors got it all.

" Well," said Uncle William, " I guess we bit off our nose to spite our face that time."

The animals all looked very glum — all but Ferdinand, who didn't care for sweets. He laughed. But Jinx said: " Well, we mustn't stop trying to think of something just because this failed. We've *got* to make them go away."

All this time it was getting closer to Christmas. Every day the eagle came with a big sack of mail in his claws containing letters that children had written to Santa Claus. They had been forwarded by the postmasters in different cities to the Postmaster General in Washington, who kept a special sack for them. Letters that didn't go through the mail, but were put up chimneys and into fireplaces by their writers, were collected by birds and passed on from claw to claw until they reached some point on the eagle's route, where he stopped and picked them up. The toy-makers in the workshops were carving and whittling and sawing and hammering and gluing and painting for dear life; and the sailors worked all day in the wrapping-room, surrounded by piles of coloured paper and bales of ribbon and big boxes of stickers, wrapping up presents. Santa Claus got his sleigh out and gave it a fresh coat of red paint and greased the runners and shined up the harness. He was a little worried about one of his reindeer, who had gone lame as the result of a fall, but the reindeer himself wasn't worried. " I'll be all right Christmas Eve," he said. " Sound as a dollar! Don't you fret, sir."

The captain had become very fond of the mice. He carried them round in his pocket and petted them all the time, and as he was very handy at carving things with a jack-knife, he had made them a little merry-go-round that they never got tired riding on. In the evening he would take them up to his room, which was fitted up like the cabin of a ship, and put them on the table, and then he would play old-fashioned waltzes and polkas and mazurkas and schottisches on his flute, and they would dance for him. Then when it was ten o'clock, he would take them to their own room and tuck them up in bed. This was a little difficult for him, as the room was so small that he could only get his head and one arm through the door, but he enjoyed doing it very much.

They particularly liked it when he took them to the meetings of the board, because then he and Mr. Pomeroy and Mr. Bashwater all made long speeches at Santa Claus. They liked Mr. Bashwater's speeches best, because he made a great many gestures and banged on the table and was so eloquent that he was always bathed in perspiration when he finally sat down. They were a little sorry for Santa Claus, who always seemed to want to know what the speeches were about. They themselves, like most people, just enjoyed the speeches, without caring what they were about.

They were a little embarrassed when the other animals asked them what had been going on. " Oh, Mr. Bashwater made a fine long speech," they'd answer.

" But what did he *say?* " Jinx would ask impatiently.

They'd think and think, and by and by Eeny would say: " We — e — ell, let me see; I guess it was about the advertising appropriation for 1931, wasn't it, Eek? Mr. Hooker wanted to use some of the big magazines, and Mr. Pomeroy said they were trying to reach children and not just people with childish minds, and then Mr. Bashwater made a long speech, and — Well, I don't know, but it was a swell speech, anyway." And so the animals knew just as much as they did before they had asked.

But sometimes the captain took the mice

down into the smoking-room where the sailors went to have what they called a night-cap before going to bed, and here they learned two very important things. The sailors sat in a big half-circle before the roaring fire, each with a cup of tea or a glass of hot milk in his hand, smoking and telling stories and munching on cookies and little sweet crackers. But all the stories were of three kinds: they were about whales, or about ghosts, or about buried treasure. When Ferdinand heard of this, he said: " H'm " several times very thoughtfully, and then he flew up on to the big chandelier in the Present Room and stood on one leg and put his head under his wing and meditated for nearly an hour.

The mice didn't think very much about it, because Ferdinand always said he was meditating when he did this, but they knew that usually it was only another way of saying that he was taking a nap. But that evening the crow called them together in a corner of the Present Room.

"I want you to tell me," he said, "just what kind of ghost-stories the sailors tell."

"Scary ones," said Eeny; and Quik said: "Awful scary ones." And Eeny said: "Mostly they're about figures in long white sheets that wail, and sometimes they're about voices that come out of the darkness, or about things that creep up behind and jump."

"H'm," said Ferdinand. "All these things take place at night, I suppose?"

"Oh, yes; late at night," said Cousin Augustus. "Goodness, I wish they wouldn't tell so many of them. I used to like to run round at night; all mice do. But now whenever I'm up after twelve, I hear footsteps coming after me and at every corner see giant cats with phosphorescent eyes."

"H'm," said Ferdinand again. "That certainly gives me an idea." So he went back and meditated again for a while, and then he called a meeting and told the animals about his plan and what he wanted each of them to do. "Go to your rooms at the usual time," he said, " just as you always do. But don't go to bed. And on the stroke of midnight we'll all meet here, and if those sailors stay here after tonight — well, my name isn't Ferdinand."

CHAPTER XIII
THE ANIMALS PLAY GHOSTS

EVERYONE in the big palace was sound asleep when the animals came one by one into the Present Room. The midnight adventure was so exciting and so funny that they laughed and whispered together until Ferdinand's " Ssssh! " quieted them. " Now no giggling," he said severely. " You know this is a serious business. It may seem like a joke, but it isn't. All ready? "

They stole down a long corridor, through an archway and across a wide court, and then up a winding stair towards the sailors' wing. Half-way up the stair they became aware of a continuous steady murmur, which rose and fell rather like the distant roar of surf on a rocky coast. It was the sailors snoring.

" My goodness," said Mrs. Wiggins, " we don't have to be very quiet."

" We'll have to do a little groaning first, to wake them up," said Ferdinand. " Mrs. W., you and the bear can do that better than the rest of us. Go up and groan outside the doors. And the rest of you be getting your costumes on and your things ready."

So the cow and the bear went up into the long hall with its many doors, behind each of which two sailors were asleep, and began to groan. They groaned low at first, but they couldn't even hear themselves above the snoring. Then they groaned louder, and louder still. And still the snoring went on uninterrupted. Even when Mrs. Wiggins let out a good full-throated bellow, it made no impression at all.

The animals didn't know what to do. " We can't scare 'em if we can't wake 'em up," said Bill.

" I can wake 'em up," said Charles. " If I crow, they'll think it's morning." So Charles crowed, and the snoring died down like the sound an airplane makes when it leaves the earth and disappears slowly in the sky, and the sound of sleepy voices came from the rooms: " Hey, Bill, time to get up." " Wake up, Ed." " Why, it's only half past twelve." " What's that noise? " " 'Tain't morning yet." And so on.

Then the six largest animals, who had dressed themselves in sheets and had false faces on, each opened one of the doors and stood on their hind legs and walked into the bedrooms, while the other animals in the hall made all the frightening noises they could think of, only not so loud that their voices would be recognized.

As soon as the sailors heard the noises and looked towards the doors and saw the tall sheeted figures with their ferocious goblin faces coming slowly towards them, they all let out terrific yells and pulled the bed-clothes up

They pulled them up so hard that their bare feet were uncovered.

over their heads. They pulled them up so hard that their bare feet were uncovered, and the animals came up to the beds and gently nipped the sailor's toes with their teeth. Then the sailors all yelled again and tumbled out of the beds and tried to get under them. But as the beds weren't very wide, there wasn't quite room for two underneath, so the sailors fought each other and tried to push each other out into the rooms. And while they were doing that, the animals went back into the hall and closed the doors softly behind them.

Mr. Pomeroy slept in a room at the head of the stairs with Mr. Bashwater. Now, each of the animals had scared two sailors, and as each sailor yelled twice, you will see that there were twenty-four yells in all. And twenty-four yells, from sailors whose throats have been toughened by the gales of the seven seas, are loud enough to wake up the soundest sleepers. So they woke Mr. Pomeroy and Mr. Bashwater.

Mr. Pomeroy came to the door and opened it. Directly in front of him he saw a huge white form whose wildly grinning face was topped by two horns. He didn't know that the form was his old friend Hank, or that the two horns were Hank's ears, for which holes had been cut in the sheet. He fell backward with a scream into the arms of Mr. Bashwater, who, as soon as Mr. Pomeroy's fall gave him an unobstructed view of the door, also fell backward, and there they lay on their backs inside the door, Mr. Pomeroy's head on Mr. Bashwater's chest.

But these two were of sterner stuff than the other sailors, and as soon as they had mustered up courage to open their eyes and saw that the door was closed and the dreadful apparition had vanished, they got up, and Mr. Pomeroy went to the speaking-tube that connected his room with Mr. Hooker's, and blew in it.

Mr. Hooker and the boatswain, Joel, slept on the floor above, and Mr. Hooker had had the speaking-tube put in so that, if any orders that he wanted to give the men occurred to him in the night, he could tell Mr. Pomeroy and have them carried out right away. So in a moment the captain's sleepy voice said hello.

" Hello, captain," gasped the mate. " Guess you'd better come down here. There's a demon or an ogre or something out in the hall; he's about ten feet high and he's got teeth as long as your hand, and I think he's et up about half the crew accordin' to the noise they been makin'."

" Eh? " said the captain incredulously. " Come, come, Mr. Pomeroy, this is no hour for jesting."

" Jesting! " exclaimed the indignant mate. " You come down and look at him and you'll see how much jest there is to it."

It took some time to convince Mr. Hooker that there was really something wrong, but when he had talked to Mr. Bashwater and found that his description of the demon agreed with the mate's, he said: " All right, all right, my men. Just wait till I get my cutlass and pistols. I'll soon settle his hash for him. Demon indeed! Cuttin' up didoes with my crew! I'll show him."

The animals were rather scared themselves now, and they retreated into the stairway. Pretty soon they heard the clump, clump of the captain's heavy sea boots coming along the corridor. " Where is he? " roared the valiant captain. " Show me your ogre! Bring on your demons! What's a demon to me? What's ten demons? Me that's fought a galleyful o' Barbary pirates to a standstill single-handed! Me that's been a mate o' Blackbeard an' Teach! Me that's tamed the wild rhinoceros till he'd eat sugar out o' my hand, an' strode into the dens o' the Bengal tiger with no weapons but my fingers and my teeth! Trot out your terrors; let's see your ten-foot-high man-eaters! Let old Hooker git his hands on 'em once, and he won't leave nothin' of 'em but a couple o' teenty weenty grease spots on the floor that ye can mop up with a lady's pocket-handkercher."

So roared the captain as he clumped down

the hall, and the animals, thoroughly frightened, crowded in the stairway, not daring to move. He came to the head of the stairs and peered down. " Are you down there, demon? " he shouted. " Come up an' rassle; come up an' git a taste o' old Doc Hooker's demon-medicine. Ye won't, hey? Well, I spose I'll have to come down to you, then."

Now, among the false faces the animals had found in the Present Room was a particularly villainous-looking Chinese mask, and Freddy had touched it up with some radium paint so that it glowed fearsomely in the dark. Cowering with the other animals in the stairway, he had kept it hidden until the captain threatened to come down. But at that threat fear overcame all the animals, and with one accord they turned to run. Someone pushed Freddy, and to keep his balance he threw up the hand that held the mask. At the same moment Cousin Augustus's nerve gave way and he had hysterics.

Hooker, peering down the dark stairs, heard

a strange tiny voice, a sort of whimpering squeak, and at the same moment was confronted by the baleful ferocity of the Chinese mask. He gave a yell — a louder yell than had yet been heard that night — dropped his cutlass, and, turning quickly, dashed back towards his room at top speed. What he did when he got there nobody knew, for he was not seen again that night, but there was a lot of dust on his coat at breakfast next morning — the kind of dust that is seldom found anywhere but under beds.

For a moment the animals were silent. Then they burst into a roar of laughter. " Good old captain! " they shouted. " ' Trot out your terrors,' eh? ' Me that's tamed the wild rhinoceros! ' It's ' Me that's run from a mouse squeak,' I guess. Can you beat that? He was scareder than any of 'em."

" That's all right," said Ferdinand. " We've done fine. But there's something still to do. There's one we haven't scared, and that's Joel. We've got to scare 'em all, you see. If there's one that hasn't been scared, he'll be brave, and he'll shame all the others into being brave and staying too. But if they're all scared, they'll all want to leave."

So they went upstairs to Joel's room. The captain's yell had waked Joel and he was sitting up in bed. Mrs. Wiggins got up on her hind legs, pulled her sheet around her, opened the door, and groaned. But the boatswain didn't yell and pull the covers over his head. He just said pleasantly: " Ah! A ghost. Come in, ghost. I've always wanted to see a ghost. Come in and sit down." And he got up out of bed and politely offered her a chair.

Mrs. Wiggins didn't know what to do. The boatswain wasn't scared at all, but she thought that if she walked slowly towards him, it might scare him, so she tried that. Unfortunately the sheet that she wore was so long that it trailed on the ground, and as she moved towards the bed, she tripped on it and fell across the chair, smashing it into kindling wood.

Joel just smiled. " That's queer," he said. " I

thought ghosts didn't weigh anything." Mrs. Wiggins scrambled to her feet and dashed out of the room, slamming the door behind her.

Out in the hall, Ferdinand was very angry. "You must have done something wrong," he said. "It ought to be easy to scare him; he isn't half so brave as the captain."

But Mrs. Wiggins was angry too. She had heard the other animals snicker when she fell over the chair. She tore off her sheet. "All right," she said. "I'm going to bed. You can scare him yourself if you're so set on it. I've had enough monkey-shines for one evening."

She was just starting for the stairs when the door opened again and Joel, in a long white night-shirt, appeared on the threshold with a candle in one hand and a pistol in the other.

"Well, upon my soul!" he exclaimed, looking from the crumpled sheet on the floor to Mrs. Wiggins. "It was the cow all the time, and not a ghost at all! Dear, dear! I have no luck at all! I did so want to see a ghost!" Then he looked round at the other animals, who still

243

had their costumes on, and his face brightened. " But perhaps these are really ghosts," he went on. " Well, there's one sure way to find out. All the story-books say that when you shoot at a ghost, the bullet goes right through him and he doesn't even notice it." And he pointed the pistol straight at the bear.

The animals weren't sure whether he really meant to shoot or not, but they weren't taking any chances, so immediately they began pulling off their sheets and throwing aside their false faces. Then, looking very much crestfallen, they filed off down the hall to the stairs. Joel watched until the last of them had disappeared; then he went back to bed.

The animals did not blame Mrs. Wiggins for the failure of their plan. After all, she had done the best she could, and it was not her fault that Joel was not afraid of ghosts. But they knew that it wasn't any use trying to scare the sailors any more. Joel would tell his story, and the sailors would be ready for them the next time, and they would get the worst of it. They would just have to think up something else.

The sailors, fortunately, took the joke in good part. They thought the animals had been very clever to play such a trick on them. Mr. Pomeroy and Mr. Bashwater were a little ashamed of having been so frightened, and they tried to get even by hiding in dark corners and jumping out and shouting " Boo! " when any of the animals went past. As for the captain, he explained a dozen times a day that he had known all along that the ghosts were just animals dressed up, and that when he had run away he had only been entering into the spirit of the thing. " I just pretended to be scared," he said. " That's what you should have done, Joel. Trouble with you is you don't know how to play. If somebody put a jack-lantern on your porch Hallowe'en night, you'd just go out and kick it to pieces. That's no way to act. Let 'em have their fun, I say."

CHAPTER XIV
THE FLIGHT OF HOOKER

FREDDY had taken very little interest in the schemes for getting rid of the sailors. He seemed to care for nothing but eating and sleeping and writing poetry. He had grown very fat, and as soon as a meal was over, he would go up to his room and lie down on the couch and take a nap. Then he would get up and lounge about and work at his verses or read until time for the next meal. His friends could seldom get him to go out skiing or coasting.

"You *ought* to get some exercise, Freddy," they would say. "All that fat can't be healthy." And they would tell him stories of pigs they had known who got so fat they burst.

246

But Freddy would just laugh. " Never felt better in my life," he would reply. " Being fat's no disgrace. Look at all the famous men who have been fat."

" But you used to be so slim and elegant and handsome," they would protest.

" Handsome is as handsome does," Freddy would say. " And if it's a choice between being handsome and a second helping of chocolate layer cake, I'll take the cake every time." And to clinch the point he would take a chocolate bar from the drawer of his desk and bite off a big piece.

One day he was sitting at his desk when Jinx pushed open the door and walked in. Any other animal would have knocked first, but Jinx's manners were never very good, for he had been badly brought up. His mother had been a handsome but very vain tabby, who spent hours keeping her fur soft and sleek, but let her kittens, of whom there were seven besides Jinx, grow up just any way. So he really couldn't be blamed for his rudeness.

Freddy frowned. " Tut, tut, Jinx," he said. " I'm glad to see you, of course, but you *must* learn to respect people's privacy. Don't you ever knock on doors? "

" Ho! " exclaimed the cat. " If I'm in the way — "

" Nonsense! " put in Freddy. " Don't be so touchy. It's all right with me. But others might not understand, and — "

" Oh, lay off, old boy," said Jinx, throwing himself down upon the sofa. " And tell us the news. I haven't seen you, except at the dinner-table, for a cat's age."

" Oh, I've been busy," said Freddy. " I tell you, Jinx, it's no easy thing being a poet. You fellows think I just dash these things off, but I tell you there's hours and hours of solid work behind every verse I turn out. Take this little thing here," and he handed a sheet of paper to his friend. " I've slaved over it until the perspiration has fairly dripped off my face."

" You could do with a little sweating," said

the cat, eyeing the stout figure that filled the easy chair from arm to arm.

" That's as may be," said Freddy. " But read it out to me, will you? I'd like to hear how it sounds."

Jinx read the poem aloud.

Contented with my earthly lot,
　My soul rejoicing sings
Until I gaze into the sky —
　Then through my mind there rings
That saddest of all earthly thoughts:
　Why do not pigs have wings?

When unimportant birds and bugs
　And bats and other things
Can soar and wheel and flit, and know
　The joy that flying brings —
Why is the pig denied the air?
　　Why do not pigs have wings?

My feet must stay upon the ground
　In all my wanderings.
Yet still desire fills all my heart
　With anxious questionings —
If even men have learned to fly,
　Why can't this pig have wings?

" Do you like it? " asked Freddy anxiously.

" Very pretty," said the cat. " How in the world you think of all these things I don't know."

" ' Things,' " repeated Freddy absently. " That's a rhyme I didn't use — Eh? Oh, you asked how I think of them. Why, they just come to me," he added modestly.

" But do you really want to fly? " asked the cat.

" Fly? Goodness, no! Why should I? "

" But that's what your poem was about."

" Oh, you don't understand," said Freddy. " That's just something I wanted in the poem, not something I really wanted. I just made myself think I wanted it so I could have something to write about."

Jinx stretched and yawned. " Well, that's beyond me. But I don't understand poetry anyway. Give me good old prose every time. Take that book I was reading yesterday, *Treasure Island*. All about pirates and buried treasure and fighting. That's some book, Freddy."

" I don't get time to read as much as I ought to," said the pig. " What's the book about? "

" I'm just telling you. There was a map — it's printed in the front of the book — that showed where some pirate treasure was buried, and a lot of these sailors were after it. Men like Hooker they were, old pirates. And then some people got it — "

But Freddy was not listening any more. Jinx went on telling the story, but the pig had picked up a pencil and was drawing something on a piece of paper.

Presently Jinx broke off and said: " Hey, you aren't listening! "

" Eh? " said Freddy, looking up. " Oh no, I'm sorry, Jinx. But what you said gave me an idea. Look here: if we draw a map like the one in that book and leave it where the sailors will find it, we'll get rid of them for good."

" Get rid of them? " said Jinx, who was sometimes rather slow. " How? "

"Why, we'll make a map of one of those islands off the coast of Florida, and we'll mark on it ' Gold here ' or ' Treasure buried here ' or something like that. You know the mice say that buried treasure is the one thing they're always interested in. If they find such a map, ten to one they'll go off to find the treasure."

As soon as Jinx got the idea, he became very enthusiastic. He went down and got the copy of *Treasure Island* he had been reading, and he and Freddy carefully drew a map something like the one in the book. They put a red cross in the middle of the island, and under it they wrote: " Dig here." They decorated the map with pictures of ships and sea serpents, and at the bottom they wrote: " This is my private map of the island where my treasure is buried. There are 400 lbs. gold, 2 qts. pigeon-blood rubies, 1 pt. diamonds, $1\frac{1}{2}$ gals. emeralds, 3 bushels mixed jewels. Packed in neat canvas containers, convenient for handling. (Signed) Capt. Kidd."

" That ought to fix 'em," said Jinx, and he

and Freddy sneaked up to Hooker's room and put the map where they were sure he would find it, between the leaves of the copy of *Alice in Wonderland* that was on his bedside table. He had a mark in at page six, and they put the map in at page eight, because although Mr. Hooker was a very slow reader, they felt sure he would at least turn the page that night.

They said nothing about their plan to the other animals, so that if it didn't come off as they expected it to, nobody but themselves would be disappointed. But they told the mice, so that if the map dropped out of the book without being noticed, they could draw the captain's attention to it.

At a quarter of twelve that night Quik came rushing down to Freddy's room. He called frantically to the gently snoring pig and even tried to shake him, but it was rather as if a man should attempt to shake the Woolworth Building. Freddy just snored on. But the mouse was desperate, so he climbed up on the bed and bit his friend sharply in the ear.

The snore ended in a squeal and a kick and a flop that brought the terrified pig out into the middle of the floor, all wrapped up in the bed-clothes. Quik was thrown into the waste-basket, and he stayed there until Freddy had stopped fighting with the bed-clothes and shouting: " Help! Murder! Somebody's stabbed me! " Then he crawled out and turned on the light and apologized for having been so brutal.

" But I had to wake you, Freddy," he said. " The captain's going away."

" Going away? " said Freddy. " That's what we wanted him to do. But couldn't you tell me in the morning instead of — "

" He's going away alone, secretly," said Quik. " After he put us to bed, we followed him back to his room. He got into bed and opened the book to read, and the map fell out. He picked it up and looked at it carefully and said ' Oho! ' several times, and then he got up and started towards the speaking-tube that goes to Mr. Pomeroy's room. He was evidently going to tell Mr. Pomeroy about the map, but then he changed his mind and began dressing. He went to the speaking-tube several times, but each time he shook his head and went back to his dressing. Then he buckled on his pistols and cutlass and put the map and his tooth-brush and shaving things and flute and bottle of hair-dye and a couple of fairy-tale books in a little suit-case and took his boots in his hand and tiptoed downstairs."

" Good heavens! " said Freddy. " I never thought he'd go alone! He's going to try to sneak off and get the treasure all for himself! That isn't what we want at all! Go find which way he's gone, Quik, and I'll wake the others. We'll meet in the Present Room."

It took some time to wake the other animals and explain to them what had happened, and by the time they were dressed and had gath-ered in the Present Room, it was nearly one o'clock, and Quik had come back and reported that Mr. Hooker had harnessed up four of the reindeer to Santa Claus's sleigh and had driven off.

Ferdinand looked very grave when he heard this. " We can't possibly catch him," he said. " Those are Santa Claus's special reindeer — the ones he uses Christmas Eve to deliver presents. They're specially trained and they're faster than anything on earth, even a fast automobile or an airplane. I'm sure I don't know what Santa Claus will say, and Christmas is only two days off."

" How could we stop him even if we did catch him? " asked Hank. " He's got his pistols. He wouldn't stop for a few animals."

" Oh, we could tell the reindeer that Santa Claus wanted them to come back," said Freddy. " They'd turn round and come back then whether Mr. Hooker wanted them to or not."

" Won't they know enough to come back anyway before Christmas Eve? " asked Robert. " They know Santa Claus can't deliver his presents without them."

" I doubt it," said Ferdinand. " Reindeer aren't over-bright, and if they think about it at all, they'll just decide that if Santa Claus hadn't wanted them to go, he wouldn't have let Mr. Hooker take them."

" Well," said Jinx at last, after they had all argued for some time without coming to any conclusion, " maybe we haven't any chance of catching up with him. I'm going to do *something*."

" So am I," said Freddy. " Go get into your furs, Jinx. Meet you in the yard."

The two animals bundled up warmly and hurried out to the stable where the rest of the reindeer were kept. With some difficulty they managed to hitch up one of the reindeer to a small sleigh that was sometimes used for racing, and started out.

They had explained to the reindeer what had happened, and had promised him an extra slab of moss — which is what reindeer eat — for his dinner, and he galloped along at a good speed, although they knew that far ahead of

257

them Mr. Hooker must be going three times as far with every stride. The tracks of his sleigh disappeared in the darkness ahead of them, lying as straight on the smooth snow as if drawn with a ruler, and the only sound was the light thudding of the reindeer's feet and the hiss of the runners gliding over the frozen surface.

" There's one chance I count on," said Jinx. " From what the mice said, the captain didn't take any food with him. He was probably afraid of waking somebody up and having to explain if he went down to the pantry. But if I know Mr. Hooker, he won't go far without stopping for food. Never saw such a man for food. He'll stop at the first igloo he comes to."

" Igloo? " said Freddy sleepily.

" Yes, one of those huts the Eskimoes make out of snow and live in. You've seen 'em time and time again."

" Oh yes, of course," said the pig. The warmth of his robes and the silence had made him sleepy, and as they went along, he murmured drowsily:

> " Oh, kindly give a mew
> When you see the first igloo.
> I'm awfully sleepy, it's true,
> But I'll wake up when you do,
> And the captain we pursue
> We'll take back to his crew,
> And as heroes then we two
> Will drive up the avenue
> And be greeted — "

" Oh, for goodness' sake, shut up! " said Jinx. But Freddy's head had fallen forward on his chest and he was asleep.

They drove on for a long time without seeing anything but snow, and the tracks of the captain's sleigh stretching across it, and at last even Jinx was beginning to nod, when the reindeer said: " Hey! Wake up! I see something ahead."

Their four eyes opened with a jerk, and, sure enough, ahead of them was a dark mass which they made out to be a sleigh, and as they approached and drew up abreast of it, they saw that one of the reindeer was lying on the snow, and the captain was vainly endeavouring to get him to his feet.

Hooker stood up and stared at them. " Hey," he said. " What's this — cats and pigs? You animals certainly do beat all, riding around in cutters just like folks! But tatter my tops'ls if you ain't come at just the right minute! " He stepped over to the side of their sleigh. " Out you go," he shouted, and, seizing Jinx in his right hand and Freddy in his left, he pulled them out, dropped them in a heap on the snow, then tossed in his suit-case, leaped in, and, smacking the reindeer on the back with the flat of his cutlass, drove off in a whirl of snow.

" He'll beat me if I don't go," called back the reindeer over his shoulder. " But I'll go as slow as I dare."

" Well," said Jinx, when they had got to their feet and brushed off the snow, " we aren't much better off than we were, but at least we've got Santa's sleigh back for him."

He went over to the reindeer who was lying on the ground. " What's the matter? " he asked.

" I was lame when we started out," said the reindeer. " My leg just gave out. Santa was trying to get it cured up by Christmas, but I guess I can't go out with him now. I can't walk on it."

" H'm," said Jinx thoughtfully. " We've got to catch the captain if we can. No use trying to unhitch you four and then hitch up three of you. The harness is too complicated for us. Tell you what we can do, though, Freddy. I think I can manage to get the harness off, and then if you're game to ride bareback, we can take two of the reindeer and follow Hooker. We can leave you here for a while, can't we? " he asked the lame reindeer. " We'll come back for you."

" Oh, sure," said the other. " I'm perfectly comfortable. Go ahead. Hope you can catch him. We'd never have taken him in the first place if we'd guessed he wasn't going on Santa Claus's business."

With a good deal of trouble they managed to get the harness off, for Jinx's claws were cold, once he took his gloves off, and Freddy's trotters were of little use. Then the reindeer had to kneel down so they could get on their backs, and off they started.

In the first mile Freddy fell off eight times, and Jinx five. Then Freddy had the idea of getting the reindeer to hold their heads back so their antlers came close to their backs. This gave something to hold on to, and after that they made good speed. It was great fun. The reindeer went like the wind; their hoofs made no noise on the snow; and in a short time Hooker was again in sight ahead of them.

" Better slow up," said Freddy. " It's no use catching up. We can't do anything yet."

So the reindeer slowed down to an easy trot, and after another hour or so they saw a little group of conical snow houses in the distance.

" Eskimos," said Freddy. " Bet you he stops to eat." And, sure enough, Hooker pulled up at the door of the largest igloo, and soon his sleigh was surrounded by a crowd of fur-clad men, women, and children.

They had hoped that he would get out and go into the igloo, but pretty soon they saw the Eskimos bringing out things for him to eat. " We'd better get up close," said Jinx. " We've got to do something now, or we'll never stop him."

Freddy slipped down from his reindeer. " I've got an idea," he said. " Edge up as close as you can, and if you see that he has caught sight of me, drive right up close to the sleigh and distract his attention."

The pig, looking in his fur coat for all the world like just another fat, roly poly little Eskimo girl, slipped unnoticed into the crowd and worked his way forward until he was close to the captain, who at that moment was reaching out the other side of the sleigh to take a large frozen fish that one of the men was handing him. Quickly Freddy reached in behind Hooker's legs under the seat and dragged out the small suit-case. If he had had hands to carry it with, he would have got away without attracting attention. But he had to take it in his mouth, and he had only wormed his way to the edge of the crowd when several of the women caught sight of him and set up a high shrill screaming. Of course they had never seen a pig before, much less a pig in a fur coat and cap, walking on his hind legs, so it is no wonder they were frightened.

Freddy ran as fast as he could to where his reindeer was kneeling down so he could get aboard. But Hooker had seen him too and had leaped from the sleigh and was pounding after him. Then Freddy tripped and fell, and the suit-case was flung several yards in front of him. He picked himself up, but it was too late to recover the case — Hooker was bending to take it up. Freddy swung himself up on the reindeer, who got up at once and started off.

But Jinx had been watching. He had moved in closer, and now he leaned forward and whispered something in his reindeer's ear. Just as Hooker bent over and reached out his hand, the reindeer, with Jinx on his back, trotted up and with a swoop of his head snatched up the suit-case on the prong of his horn and galloped triumphantly away. At the same moment, at a shout from Freddy, the reindeer that was hitched to the sleigh also galloped off, and Hooker was left alone in the Eskimo village. As they headed back north at top speed, Jinx looked over his shoulder. The captain, surrounded by a crowd of wondering Eskimos, was dancing up and down in fury, shaking his fists after the vanishing animals. Then, just before the distance got too great for Jinx to see what was going on, Hooker snatched off his hat, flung it on the ground, and jumped on it with both feet.

CHAPTER XV
CHRISTMAS EVE AT SANTA'S

It was late in the afternoon when Jinx and Freddy finally got back to the palace. Santa Claus laughed until the tears ran down his fat red cheeks when he heard their story.

"I don't know what I'll do when you animals leave me and go back to your homes," he said. "We've always had a good time up here on the top of the world, but since you've been here, it has been twice as much fun. Well, well, the poor old captain! I should like to have seen his face! But I'm afraid it serves him right for taking the reindeer without my permission. I

266

must send out and bring Blixen in, I suppose. I'm sorry his leg has given out, for tomorrow night is Christmas Eve, and there isn't another reindeer I can put in his place on the sleigh. They're fairly fast, some of them, but they're not sure-footed enough, and a reindeer has to be sure-footed to keep from falling when he gets on some of those steep, snow-covered roofs."

" Why couldn't you put Uncle William in his place, sir? " asked Freddy. " He's fairly fast for a horse — of course nothing like your reindeer, but he used to be in a circus, and from what he's told us about the tricks he had to do, I'm sure he'd have no trouble in keeping his feet on the steepest roof."

" Why, that's a fine idea, Freddy," said Santa Claus. " I never thought of it. I did think Bill might do, because a goat is used to climbing; but he's so much smaller than the reindeer that I'm afraid he'd look funny hitched up with them. The children wouldn't like it if Santa Claus came with three reindeer and a

267

goat. Well, now, why didn't I ever think of that? You two go in and get something to eat; you must be pretty hungry. And ask Uncle William to come out and see me."

Freddy and Jinx went in and ate a huge lunch, and then they took Mr. Hooker's suitcase up to his room. But before they left it, they took out the map. " We mustn't leave that here," said Jinx. " He'll just try to get away with it again if we do."

" Tear it up," said Freddy.

" No," replied the cat, " I'll hide it somewhere. I have an idea we can use it yet."

Late that evening an Eskimo brought the captain back to the palace on a dog-sled. Mr. Hooker seemed very grumpy, and he went straight to his room without speaking to anybody. He came down to breakfast the next morning, but only answered with grunts when spoken to, and between courses sat and twirled his moustaches and glared down the long dining-room at the animals. When the mice had finished their breakfast, they went

Freddy and Jinx went in and ate a huge lunch

over to his table, but instead of picking them up he merely glowered angrily at them, then jumped to his feet, shook his fist at them, shouted: " Traitors! " in a loud voice, and went back to his room, where he remained until lunch, playing strange wild music on his flute.

But as it was the day before Christmas, everybody in the palace was very busy, and nobody had time to wonder about the captain. The thousands and thousands of presents were stacked up in the courtyard, ready to be loaded into the sleigh and the pack that Santa Claus carries on his back. A lot of last-minute letters were being hastily opened and presents wrapped and addressed for the children who had written them. And the animals and the sailors and all the workmen in the toy-factory were hanging up their own stockings and decorating trees and getting presents ready for each other. And in the midst of all this hurry and bustle, Santa Claus had found time to hitch up Uncle William with the three reindeer and give him a try-out round the yard and over the palace roofs.

" I don't see how he manages to deliver all these presents," said Mrs. Wiggins. She and Mrs. Wogus were wrapping up some dog-biscuits in red paper to put in Robert's stocking.

" It isn't really as much work as it looks," said Mrs. Wogus, " though it's enough, land knows! I've had it all explained to me. You see, he tries to deliver all the presents as near twelve o'clock as he can. When it's twelve o'clock in New England, it's only eleven in Ohio, and out on the Pacific coast it's still early in the evening, and in Japan it is still noon of the day before."

" Eh? " exclaimed Mrs. Wiggins. " What are you talking about, sister! If it's twelve o'clock, it's twelve o'clock. I never heard — "

" Oh, you don't understand," said Mrs. Wogus. " I could show you if I had a globe. What I mean is, the earth goes round, and the sun comes up on New England before it does on California, doesn't it? And when it's shining on Mr. Bean's farm, it's dark in Japan, isn't it? "

" I guess so," said Mrs. Wiggins doubtfully. " It sounds all right when you say it, but when I begin to think about it, it makes my head feel funny."

" You don't want to think about it," said her sister. " You just see how it is, and then it's perfectly simple. Santa Claus delivers his presents in New England at twelve o'clock. An hour later he gets to Ohio. But it isn't one o'clock there, it's only twelve. He goes round the whole world the same way. He delivers all his presents at midnight, but he has twenty-four hours to do it in."

" Oh dear! " said Mrs. Wiggins. " Don't tell me any more. You've got me all confused now. See here, are we going to give Henrietta this china egg with the forget-me-nots on it, or the bottle of Jockey Club perfume? "

" I think she'd like the perfume best. Wrap it up and I'll get a card ready. Where are the stickers? "

Mrs. Wogus didn't try to explain any more, and it is doubtful if Mrs. Wiggins ever really understood about the change of time, although she was not to blame for that, as she had never been to school and had lived all her life on a very small farm. Nor did it really matter, for she understood so many things that were more important, such as how to be nice to animals who were in trouble, and what to say to stop animals' being angry at each other.

As soon as everything was ready, Santa Claus set out. He had fastened a pair of antlers to Uncle William's head so that the horse would look as much as possible like a reindeer. Uncle William was very proud to be going with Santa Claus. It was the most wonderful thing that had ever happened to him. He had raced a good deal when he was younger, but he had never even imagined such speed as he made that night. He never knew afterwards quite how it happened, whether the reindeer pulled him along or whether there was some magic about it. His hoofs seemed to skim the snow.

They sped through the forest so fast that the trees fairly whizzed backward past them, like the pickets on a fence that you pass in a swift automobile. Soon the forest was behind, and houses began to appear. A leap, and they were on a roof; Santa was out of the sleigh and down the chimney and back again in the sleigh almost before they had come to a stop — and then another leap, and in a swirl of snow they were off again. Through towns and villages and cities, up narrow mountain roads, across bridges, over cultivated valleys, along beaches where the surf broke white in the starlight, they raced, faster and faster; passing lighted trains that seemed to be standing still, though they were making their fifty miles an hour; passing speeding automobiles whose occupants caught but a glimpse of them as they hurried by and were never sure afterwards of the reality of what they had seen. After a little it was all like a dream to Uncle William; he galloped and galloped, and lights and buildings and woods and fields whizzed by in a confused mass; and he could hear Santa Claus humming a little tune to himself as he pulled the reins gently, now to the left, now to the right, to guide their flight. The horse didn't seem to get tired, either, for all the swiftness of the pace. It was too exciting, he was too proud of his part in it, to feel fatigue. And when at last he was back in the stable, and his harness was taken off and a good feed of oats was brought to him, he was sorry that it was all over.

" Splendid work! " said Santa Claus, patting him on the shoulder. " If it weren't for you, there'd be a lot of unhappy children to-morrow morning who'd be wondering why I'd forgotten them. And you never slipped once. Even I lost my footing on that steep slate roof in Minneapolis, and if I hadn't caught hold of the chimney, you'd have had to dig me out of the snow-drift at the side of the house." He shook with laughter. " That's happened to me more than once, I can tell you. You'd be surprised at some of the things that have happened. Once I fell through a skylight right into a bed where four children were trying to keep awake so they could see me when I came down the chimney. They saw me all right, and felt me. I nearly squashed them."

" You must have had lots of funny experiences," said the horse.

" I have. I'll tell you about them some time. But now I think we both want to get to bed. There'll be lots of eating and excitement tomorrow, and we want to be rested."

Christmas at Santa Claus's palace was, as you may imagine, nothing but fun and happiness for all the animals and people under that generous roof. It would take much too long to tell of the presents they exchanged, and the turkeys and plum puddings and mince pies and candy they ate, and the games they played. Even Mr. Hooker recovered from his anger and disappointment sufficiently to eat an enormous dinner — for which he dressed in full pirate costume — cocked hat, gold-laced coat, ear-rings, red sash, and all — and to play for them afterwards on his flute while they all danced.

The dancing was really worth seeing. The sailors danced hornpipes and jigs; the ship's carpenter, Mr. McTavish, put on kilts and danced a Highland fling; Mr. Bashwater did the harpooner's jig, which is something like the gimpus dance, with many complicated figures; and even the captain finally consented to do his famous and very graceful dance to Mendelssohn's *Spring Song,* for which he wore a leopard-skin and a green wreath, and carried a basket of artificial crocuses. The animals danced too, mostly old-fashioned round dances. Mrs. Wogus in particular turned out to be a really fine dancer. Her polka was quite astonishing.

Late in the evening, when the merriment was at its height, there was one unpleasant incident. One of the sailors, a greedy and ill-tempered man named Pell, was complaining about the present his room-mate, Mr. Osnip, had given him. " It's all very well to talk about the Christmas spirit," he was saying. " But Jim Osnip hasn't got it. He just simply hasn't got it, that's all! Why I gave him a swell ivory manicure set, and what did he give me? A couple of miserable little guest-towels. Why, they're not even linen! And look, here's the price tag — he didn't even take it off — nineteen cents! What kind of a present is that to give your mate? "

Some of the sailors had gathered round, and Mr. Bashwater said: " Why, Pell, I think those are very nice towels. Jim hasn't got very much money, you know, and he's spent a lot of time embroidering your monogram on them. See here — "

" I don't care about that at all," said Pell crossly. " What I say is — "

But just then Mr. Osnip himself pushed through the ring. " You don't like 'em, eh? " he said. " All right, give 'em back. Here's your old manicure set. Give me those towels! " And he started to pull them away from his friend.

But Mr. Pell didn't really want to give up

the towels, so he hung on to them, and they tugged and pulled until at last one of the towels gave way and tore down the middle, leaving Mr. Pell lying on his back with half a towel in his hand, and Mr. Osnip lying on *his* back with a towel and a half in *his* hand.

The disturbance had brought everyone together in that corner of the Present Room. Freddy had been upstairs fixing up something on his typewriter, and now, as he came down with a sealed envelope in his mouth, Jinx came up to him and said: " You're just in time. Now's the time to give it to him."

Freddy nodded and pushed his way through the crowd. Mr. Hooker had just taken matters in hand and was scolding the two sailors, who stood before him blushing and with downcast and shamefaced looks. The pig stood on his hind legs and offered the envelope to the captain.

" What's this? " said Mr. Hooker.

The sailors all looked over his shoulder as

he turned the envelope over in his hands. " It says something on it," said one of them.

" Eh? So it does. ' The contents of this letter are of interest to the officers and crew of the *Mary Ann*.' H'm, wonder what can be in it."

" Why don't you open it and find out? " suggested someone.

" That's an idea," said Hooker, and tore open the envelope. Out dropped a folded paper.

Hooker had recognized it immediately as the treasure map, and he stooped to snatch it up before anyone else should see what it was. But Mr. Osnip was quicker, and in a few moments every sailor in the room knew what it was and they all crowded closer about the captain, who, realizing now that it was useless to try to keep it for himself, and knowing that the animals could not give him away, pretended that he had known what it was all the time.

" It's a little surprise I've had in store for you for some time, men," he said. " I found this several days ago, but I knew if I told you about it then, you'd want to start right away to hunt for the treasure, so I thought I'd wait until Christmas was over. Santa Claus would have been hurt if we'd left before Christmas. And then I thought it would make a nice Christmas surprise for you. It's my Christmas present to all of you."

At this there was a burst of prolonged cheering. "Hurray! Hurray! Three cheers for Mr. Hooker! And for Captain Kidd's treasure!"

"Now what I think we ought to do," went on the captain, "is to pack our suit-cases and set out tonight. We don't want anybody else to get to the treasure ahead of us, and although it has been where it is for over a hundred years, you never can tell how much longer it may stay there. We don't know how many other maps like this are in existence. So get your stuff ready, and then say good-bye to Santa Claus, and don't forget to thank him for the nice time you've had and for all the nice presents, and we'll get on our way."

After another fit of cheering the sailors scattered to their rooms to pack.

" Well, I guess we fixed that all right," said Freddy.

" I'll say we did," replied the cat. " They've forgotten all about reorganizing Santa Claus's business already. He'll be pretty glad, I bet."

" Yes," said Freddy, " but I expect we'd better tell him about the map."

" I suppose we ought to," replied Jinx.

So they went into Santa Claus's study and told him the whole story.

Santa Claus was not at all angry with them, and he was amused at their cleverness, but he looked at the same time rather worried. " I'm pleased that you've taken so much trouble for me," he said, " and it's true that I'd be glad to have the sailors go. They are nice men and I like them, but their ideas about business are very upsetting. I thought at first that their way of doing things might make my work here easier, and in some ways it did, but I think, after all, I prefer the old-fashioned way of doing things. Everybody was happy, and, after all, that's the main thing.

" Nevertheless I don't see how we can let them go like this. It isn't really quite honest, is it, to let them take a long, hard journey, and spend months of their time hunting for something that we know doesn't exist? "

" No — o — o," said Freddy slowly. " I don't suppose it is. But — "

" There isn't really any ' but ' about it," said Santa Claus. " You agree with me, you see. I think we'll have to tell them."

" Oh, but, gosh! " protested Jinx. " Excuse me, sir, but I mean, isn't there anything else we can do? Don't you know of any real treasure they could hunt for? If we could only — "

" Wait! " exclaimed Santa Claus. " That gives me an idea, Jinx. It certainly gives me an idea! Our objection is that there isn't any treasure on the island you drew the map of, isn't it? But suppose we put a treasure there, eh? Suppose I harnessed up the reindeer and drove down there and planted a treasure for

283

them to dig up? That would fix it, wouldn't it? "

The animals were delighted with this scheme. But when it came to carrying it out there were some difficulties. On the maps they had made a list of the treasure: four hundred pounds of gold and several bushels of precious stones. " I'm a pretty rich man," said Santa Claus, " but even I couldn't get together as big a treasure as that. Still, I guess we could arrange that. The main thing is that they shan't be disappointed with what they find. I'll get together enough valuables so they'll all have plenty of money to live on comfortably for the rest of their lives. And then I'll drive down there and bury it in a day or two. — Ah, here they come to say good-bye to me," he said, as the thump of heavy sea boots was heard outside in the hall.

" We oughtn't to be staying much longer ourselves," said Robert as the animals stood in the courtyard and waved good-bye to the sailors, who straggled out of the gate, each with a suit-case bulging with the presents he had received in one hand, and a handkerchief in the other which he turned to wave every few steps, for they were all sorry to go.

" I suppose you're right," said Hank. " Mr. Bean is probably pretty worried about us, although Santa Claus told me the other day that he'd sent him a letter to say that we were all right."

" Well, for my part," said Henrietta, " I'll be glad to get back. I've got my children to bring up, and my work to do — goodness knows what state that coop is in now, for Leah's a good girl, but she's no housekeeper. And all this traipsing round the country and having a good time is all very well, but I was brought up to think that work was of some use in the world too. And I expect you were too, Hank."

" Yes, I expect I was," replied the horse, " though I don't think a little fun ever hurt anybody."

" A *little* fun — certainly. But there's been

nothing but fun and games and cuttin' didoes for months. Now I say it's time we sobered down and did some work."

" Oh, you and your work, Henrietta," said Jinx, who was the only one of the animals who ever dared talk back to the hen. " You make me tired. Loosen up and shake a leg once in a while. Do a little dance or sing a song or turn a somersault or something. It'd do you good. And what work are you going to do here? "

" There's work enough waiting for all of us at home," she said crossly.

" Sure, but home's a long way off. In the mean time why not have what fun you can? Not just be an old sour face."

" Humph! " grunted the hen. " Who cares what an old bald-headed cat says! If you'd — "

" Oh, come," said Hank, " let's not quarrel. — Listen! The sailors have stopped and they're singing *Good night, Ladies*."

The sound of the song floated to them through the cold air from where, far off now on the broad snow-field, the sailors were grouped about their captain, who was leading them with his flute. They sang the song, gave a final cheer, waved their handkerchiefs once more, then turned and plodded on out of sight.

But Freddy took up the tune. " Good-bye, sailors," he sang,

" Good-bye, sailors,
Good-bye, sailors,
We're glad to have you go.
Merrily you slide along, slide along, glide along,
Merrily you glide along
O'er the deep white snow."

CHAPTER XVI

THE RIDE HOME

" I'll tell you what I'm going to do," said Santa Claus. They were sitting round the fire after dinner, two days after the sailors had gone. " I know you animals feel you ought to be getting back home, so I'm not going to try to keep you. But it's a long trip on foot back to Mr. Bean's farm. Now, out in the stable is a big sleigh that we use sometimes for sleigh-ride parties. It will hold twenty-five people, so I guess it's big enough for you all to be comfortable. I'll hitch up a dozen or so of the racing reindeer to it and take you all back home. Of course we won't go so fast as I can go with the little sleigh on Christmas Eve, but we'll make better time than an automobile could, or even a train. And you'll be home to celebrate New Year's with the Beans."

The animals said at first oh no, they couldn't think of having him go to all that trouble, and it was asking too much, and so on; but he had made up his mind. So the next morning they packed up and went out into the courtyard, where the sleigh was waiting. Santa Claus sat on the driver's seat with the twenty-four reins of red leather in his hands, and Ella and Everett, one on each side of him; and the animals packed themselves in and burrowed down in the warm straw in the body of the sleigh, and they set off.

For the first hour or so nobody said much of anything. They all felt rather sad at leaving the pleasant little bedrooms and all the comforts they had enjoyed, and they had already begun to miss the jolly meals in the big dining-room and the long, happy days playing games outdoors and in the Present Room, and the cosy evenings about the fire, when they talked quietly and Santa Claus told stories. But after a while their spirits revived and they laughed and sang and joked as the winter landscape raced past them, and the steel runners whined over the snow.

At the end of the first day they camped by the little lake on which stood the house where Ella and Everett had once lived. When supper was over and they were all gathered about the big fire of wood that they had collected in the forest, Santa Claus walked across the frozen lake to the house and rapped on the door.

" Come in, come! " called a harsh, impatient voice.

He opened the door and walked in. There beside the table sat Kate and Pete, Kate busy with some sewing, Pete studying his grammar. They both looked up and scowled.

" Good evening," said Santa Claus pleasantly. " You're Kate and Pete, I suppose? "

" Yeah," said Kate, " just for the sake of

the argument, I suppose we are, and I suppose you're Santy Claus."

"That's just who I am, as a matter of fact," replied the saint.

"Oh, sure," said Kate, "and I'm Cinderella, and this is my friend the King of the Cannibal Island, and — "

"Suppose we see what the gentleman wants," interrupted Pete.

Kate scowled more deeply than ever, but she stopped talking, and Santa Claus said: "I came to speak to you about Ella and Everett, who used to live here."

They both jumped up at that, and Kate said eagerly: "You seen 'em? You know where they are?"

"Yes," Santa replied, "they're safe and comfortable. But they're not coming back here. You're not fit to look after those children, and so — "

"Oh, we aren't, hey?" demanded Kate furiously, looking round for her broom. "Well, let me tell you something, Mr. Whatever-your-name-is. If you've got them children, you bring 'em back here quick, if you want to keep out of trouble. There's a law in this country against kidnappers, and if you don't watch out, you'll find yourself in jail." She turned quickly on Pete. "Why don't *you* do somethin'? You're a man, ain't you? Tell him he's got to bring them children back. Don't just stand there and take all his sass."

" 'Sass' is not in Webster," remarked Pete. " And I suggested before that we listen to what he has to say. Then if it is necessary, I shall do something."

"Very sensible," said Santa Claus. "I think you will be satisfied with what I have to say." He fumbled under his coat and drew out a fat pocket-book, from which he counted down on the table a number of bills. " This money," he said, " is yours if you give up all claim to the children."

Kate put her hand over the money before she had counted it. " 'Tain't enough! " she shouted. " Tryin' to buy my dear children from me that I cherish like the apple of my eye! You old varmint! ”

“ ‘ Varmint,’ ” said Pete, “ is a colloquialism not generally used in polite circles. And suppose we count the money.” He proceeded to do so. “ Very generous, I think,” he said.

But Kate was not satisfied. “ ’Tain’t enough! ” she repeated. “ Double it! Double it or get out! ”

“ Oh, very well,” said Santa, reaching for the money.

But at this Kate backed down. “ Well,” she said, “ perhaps I was a mite hasty. I love them children like the — ”

“ Like the apple of your eye,” said Santa Claus. “ Quite so. And now that that is settled, I wish you a very good evening.”

As he closed the door, he heard Kate shout: “ Gimme them bills! ” and Pete replied: “ ‘ Those ’ would be more correct usage.” And then there was a sound of whacking. Kate was using her broomstick.

They slept by the lake that night, and the next morning, bright and early, they were off again. Pretty soon the woods gave way to farming country, and then larger and larger villages appeared. At noon they whizzed across the long bridge over the Saint Lawrence River so fast that the customs men never even saw them go by, and then they were in the United States again. By four o'clock they were nearly home, and they were all leaning out excitedly and pointing out to each other familiar landmarks.

"Here's Centerboro," they shouted, as the snowy road plunged down a hill and between a long double line of big elm-trees that bordered the main street.

Nobody paid any attention to the shrill whistle that was repeated several times as they passed the Town Hall, but a block or two farther on a tall man with a silver star on the breast of his overcoat sprang out into the path of the swiftly approaching sleigh. "Stop!" he shouted. "Stop, I tell ye!"

Santa Claus sawed on the reins and brought the reindeer prancing and snorting to a stop in a smother of flying snow.

" It's a speed trap," said Hank. " They catch a lot of autos going too fast in the summer-time, I've heard."

" But they can't stop Santa Claus! " exclaimed the other animals.

The man, who had a very red face and a little beard that waggled when he talked, came up to the side of the sleigh. " You stop when I tell ye to! " he shouted angrily. " You fellers seem to think ye own the county, so ye do. But I'll show ye! I arrest ye for breakin' the speed limit, and ye're comin' with me to the Jestice of the Peace."

" The speed limit is for automobiles," said Santa Claus. " This isn't an automobile."

" Is that so! " replied the constable. " Goin' to give me an argument, be ye? Come along here all dressed up in a red suit with the outlandishest rig I ever see in my born days, and give me an argument, me, Henry Snedeker, that's been constable in this town since before you was in long clothes. Well, I arrest ye fer exceedin' the speed limit, and fer disturbin' the peace, and fer — "

He stopped suddenly and his mouth fell open, and he began edging away in alarm. He had been standing close to the side of the sleigh, but had paid no attention to its occupants. The animals were all getting angry, and at last the bear leaned over the side and put his nose close to the constable's face and gave a deep bass growl.

"What ye got in there, animals?" demanded the constable. "A menagerie, eh? A circus! Ye can't operate a circus in this town without a licence. I arrest ye for operatin' a circus without a licence, too."

The anger in his voice was somewhat mixed with fear now, but he still stood his ground, and began lugging an old-fashioned horse-pistol out of his pocket.

"I'll go to the Justice of the Peace with you," said Santa Claus, "if you'll tell me where he is.

If you only want to make a speech, I'm going on, for I'm in a hurry."

" You'll go on when I tell ye to," replied Mr. Snedeker. He tried to cock the ancient pistol, but it had rusted so badly that even when he put the butt on the ground and held the barrel in both hands and tried to force back the hammer with his foot, he had no success. And while he was still struggling with it, the bear jumped out of the sleigh, seized him about the waist in his powerful grip, and tossed him in among the other animals, who promptly sat upon him.

Santa Claus laughed heartily. " Now," he said, " if you'll tell me where the Justice of the Peace lives, I'll drive there, and we'll have this settled."

" An' I arrest ye for assault an' battery," the muffled voice went on from the bottom of the sleigh, " an' fer unprovoked attack, an' — "

" The Justice of the Peace is three doors down, on the right," said Hank. " But why don't you just let us throw him out in the snow and go on, sir? They'll probably fine you and delay you half a day."

" No," said Santa Claus, " that would be breaking the law. We don't want to do that. I can fix it all right." And so he drove on and was presently ringing the Justice's door-bell.

The door was opened by a little old woman in black, and Santa entered and the animals trooped after him, the bear carrying the still protesting constable.

The Justice of the Peace was a small dried-up little man in black, with steel spectacles pushed up on his forehead. He rose from behind a black-walnut desk where he had been taking a nap. " What's this — what's this? " he spluttered as the strangely assorted crowd pushed into the room. " What's the meaning of this, sir? "

The constable, released by the bear, told his story. " They were going at least fifty miles an hour," he said.

" We were going at least a hundred," put in Santa Claus.

" What, what, what? " exclaimed the magistrate. " You *admit* going at such a dangerous rate of speed? "

" Certainly," said Santa Claus.

" Twenty-five dollars," said the magistrate. " Now as to these other charges — assault and battery, obstructing the public highway, operating a menagerie without a licence, illegal entry, arson — "

" Wait a minute," said the saint. " I haven't had time to commit all these offences. I've only been in your town about three minutes."

" That will have to be proved," said the Justice of the Peace. " Your name? "

" Santa Claus."

The magistrate stared at him. " You are choosing a poor time to joke," he said severely.

" Perjury and contempt of court," said the constable.

" Nevertheless, that *is* my name," said Santa Claus.

" Well, well," said the Justice of the Peace,

" it's possible, of course. Let it pass. Somebody else *might* have that name. Age? "

" Eight hundred years, roughly," replied the saint.

" Eight hun — Say, look here, mister," burst out the constable, " you'll get eight hundred years in jail — ' roughly ' too — if there's any more of this. Your honour — "

" Yes, yes, yes," said the magistrate testily, " take him off to jail, Henry. Maybe a night in the town cooler will make him see sense."

" One moment," said Santa Claus. " I have given you my right name and my right age. I can prove it to you in three minutes."

The constable and the magistrate looked at each other with raised eyebrows, and the constable winked. There was a silence through which the voice of the little old woman could be heard complaining. " All these nasty animals traipsing through my clean front hall and tracking up the floor with their great muddy feet! "

" All right," said the Justice of the Peace. " I'll give you three minutes."

" Good," said the saint with a smile. " We'll take you first, Constable Henry Snedeker. You're about sixty-five years old. On the 23rd of December fifty-six years ago you wrote a letter to Santa Claus asking for a jack-knife. You got the jack-knife in your stocking, along with two oranges, a jumping-jack, two Jackson balls, and a stick of peppermint candy. Am I right? "

The constable fell back against the wall. " Consarn ye! " he exclaimed in angry amazement, " ye are Santa Claus after all! And to think of all the things ye've stuffed in my stocking when I was a little shaver, and I go and arrest ye fer speedin'! Well, sir, I'll be dosh heckled! "

But the Justice of the Peace was not convinced. " Come, brace up, Henry," he said. " You know your memory ain't what it was. How do *you* know what you had in your stocking fifty-six years ago? Every boy has had a knife and those other things given him at some time. Your memory's playing you tricks."

" No," said Santa Claus, " Mr. Snedeker's memory is remarkably clear. Now, your honour, I will refresh yours. Your name is Philemon Prendegast. You're sixty-eight years old. When you were fourteen, your sister, who let us in and is now standing there in the doorway, was ashamed of you because you still played with dolls. On Christmas Eve 1876 I put in your stocking, as you had requested, a French doll with long yellow — "

" Stop, stop! " shouted the magistrate, jumping to his feet with a very red face. " You're crazy! Get out of here, all of you! Out, out! Your fine is remitted — "

The constable had doubled up with laughter in a chair. " Dolls! " he roared. " Ho! That's a good one, that is! Wait till the boys down to the store get hold of that one! Old Squire Prendegast playin' with — " He choked on a howl of merriment, and the bear had to slap him on the back before he could get his breath back.

The little old lady in black had come forward and bobbed an old-fashioned curtsy to Santa Claus. " I'm very pleased to meet you," she said. " To think of all the Christmas Eves I sat up and held my eyelids open with my fingers so I could get a glimpse of you, and now I see you for the first time. You always came after I had dropped off to sleep. But, sir, please don't say anything about Philemon and the dolls to anybody else. 'Twan't his fault he played with 'em, and anyway — "

" Anyway it wasn't any harm," interrupted Santa Claus. " You're quite right. I shan't say anything about it to anybody. And Mr. Snede-ker," he added, turning to the constable, who was wiping his eyes, " I think, if I were you, I wouldn't say anything about it either. I never threaten, but I know you're pretty fond of peace and quiet in your home, and it would be too bad if those active little grand-children of yours should get a lot of drums and whistles and tin horns next Christmas, wouldn't it?"

The constable looked somewhat crestfallen. "I s'pose 'twould," he said. "Gosh, there's little enough happens in this town, and then a good story comes along and I can't tell it. But I won't. I promise you, sir."

So Santa Claus said good-bye to the Prendegasts and Mr. Snedeker, and they went out and got into the sleigh and drove on. And in fifteen minutes the sleigh was the centre of a shouting, happy mob of animals in the Beans' driveway, and Mr. and Mrs. Bean had shaken hands with Santa Claus and hugged all the animals and kissed the children and patted the reindeer and accepted Santa Claus's invitation to come up to the north pole and spend next Christmas with him. And Mr. Bean had made a short speech.

It wasn't a very good speech, for Mr. Bean was not a practised public speaker; indeed, he wasn't much of a private speaker either, and sometimes a whole day would go by without his having said anything but " Please pass the potatoes," or something like that. But his speech was very much appreciated. First he thanked Santa Claus for having taken such good care of the animals, who, he said, were the finest lot of animals on any farm, in any county, in any state, in the whole country. There weren't any words, he said, to express how glad he was to have them back. And they'd brought back with them, he said, the one thing he and Mrs. Bean had always wanted — the two children. Now, he said, they had something to work for and bring up and leave the farm to.

And then he took off his hat and threw it up in the frosty air and gave three cheers for everybody, in which Santa Claus and the children and the animals all joined, and then he lit his pipe and hoisted Everett on his shoulder and stumped off into the house to show the little boy a model of a windmill that he had once carved with his jack-knife. And Mrs. Bean showed Santa Claus into the parlour and gave him yesterday's Centerboro *Gazette* to read while she was getting supper ready. And the animals showed the bear his new home, and then all went into the cow-barn for a good long gossip. And everybody was thoroughly and completely happy.

And as there is very little to write about either people or animals when they are thoroughly and completely happy (except to say that they *are* thoroughly and completely happy), this is the end of the story.